What We Build Upon the Ruins

What We Build Upon the Ruins

and other stories

Giano Cromley

Tortoise Books

Chicago, IL

FIRST EDITION, NOVEMBER, 2017

Published in the United States by Tortoise Books

www.tortoisebooks.com

ASIN: B0755KC38M
ISBN-10: 0-9986325-5-4
ISBN-13: 978-0-9986325-5-1

Cover image via Shutterstock

Cover design by Daniela Campos

Author Photo by Jeff Bohmann

Tortoise Books Logo Copyright ©2017 by Tortoise Books.
Original artwork by Rachele O'Hare.

For Natalie

When the angels come, they'll cut you down the middle, to see if you're still there. To see if you're still there.

—Cloud Cult

Contents

What We Build Upon the Ruins

Dad wasn't what you'd call "handy," and Mom wasn't the type to "go with the flow," so it's hard to say how we ended up spending several weekends during the summer of 1989 making a birchbark canoe on Michigan's Upper Peninsula.

"It'll be a bonding experience," he said one night, waving the brochure over the dinner table. He said this as if it were still up for discussion, though he'd already sent in the deposit. "This'll be good for the family. Teach the boys the value of hard work."

Marty and I exchanged anxious glances across the table.

"Plus, we'll end up with a hand-made wooden canoe at the end of the summer," he added.

"You've never paddled a canoe in your life," Mom pointed out.

"They don't make them like that anymore," Dad said, shaking his head appreciatively. "They just don't."

"It's not going to replace what we lost," Mom said, her voice very quiet now. "Making something doesn't fix anything."

"It might help us be less self-absorbed," Dad said.

No one said anything else after that.

≈

Starting in June, every weekend we'd load up the Gran Torino with coolers and tents and sleeping bags and bug spray. Marty and I sat in the way back, so we didn't have to listen to books on tape. We'd occupy ourselves by reading comics until we got carsick. Then we'd play the license plate game, though we never saw more than a dozen different states on the four-hour drive.

I was eleven. Marty was almost ten. As his older brother, I was supposed to protect him from the perils of childhood. But because we were so close in age, we figured things out together mostly.

There was nothing wrong with Marty. He was small. The doctors said he always would be. And he was just reaching that age when it started to matter. His main coping strategy was cardboard boxes. Whenever Marty felt anxious or scared, he'd go down to the basement and climb into one. The first time I found him there it was a couple weeks after the accident.

"What's going on?" I asked, folding back the cardboard flap.

"I'm thinking," he said.

"I know. But why here?"

Marty's big eyes peered out at me from the darkness of the box. "I think Mom wishes I was a girl."

"Why do you think that?" I asked, though I already knew.

It was quiet between us for a moment. I could hear our parents' raised voices coming through a vent somewhere overhead.

"I made up a new comic book character," Marty said, suddenly hopeful. "His name is The Human Hologram."

"What's his power?"

"He does this thing where he's there, but he's not really there."

"I don't get it," I said. "How is that a super power?"

Marty looked nervous, like he'd revealed something he shouldn't have. "The cardboard makes me calm," he said, putting his hands against the sides of the box. "The smell reminds me of something happy, but I can't remember what."

≈

Angus Boudreaux was three-quarters Anishinaabe and claimed to be one of the last surviving tribal members who knew how to make a traditional birchbark canoe. The first day we assembled in the woody acreage behind his trailer, he told us to call him Big Angus.

He was six foot six, with a choppy mullet and a red-checked woodsman's cap and a fraying tweed jacket. His glasses were so thick his eyes looked like peepholes.

"*Annii, zhaagnaash.*" He smiled and chuckled to himself for a second. "That means, 'Welcome, friends.' Over the next several weekends, I'll be showing you how to make *weegwasi jeemon* the way my people have done since the olden days."

Three other groups showed up that first day. The Wetzels were a family of five with three daughters, the middle of whom seemed to be roughly my age. The Caspers were a family of four, with two sons who were a little younger than Marty. The last group consisted of five men in their thirties who had all belonged to the same fraternity at the University of Michigan.

"In the olden days," Big Angus said, "making a canoe was a family project. It has to be a group that can work together and stick together." Here, Big Angus looked us over, as if checking for weakness.

"First thing we gotta do is get ourselves the bark," he went on. "So me and Eugene—" Big Angus pointed to a wiry guy with a thin mustache who had been standing behind us, "—we found ourselves a good grove of white birch."

Eugene made a follow-me gesture and set off into the woods. The going quickly became uncomfortable.

"How far is it, Michael?" Mom asked. "I'm wearing sandals."

My father glanced around at the others. It was clear we were the group least prepared for the day's rigors.

"It builds character," he said.

Then I heard my mom make a sound that I can't really describe but usually meant she was upset.

≈

It turned out we only had to walk ten more minutes. We'd entered a different part of the forest. The trees were white with black striations, and their leaves let in a lot more of the sun. The air felt lighter, cleaner.

Eugene gave each group a hooked knife and instructed us to find a suitable tree. We settled on one that was so thick I couldn't put my arms around it.

"Before you make a cut," Eugene said, "it's important to know this will kill the tree."

Mom gasped. Marty looked like he wanted to find a cardboard box to hide in.

"The elders tell us we have to ask the tree's permission first." He nodded solemnly. "So go ahead."

We looked at each other. I could tell none of us wanted to do it.

"You're holding the knife," Mom said to Dad, by which I think she meant: This was your idea in the first place.

My dad stepped up and laid his hand on the trunk. "Well, tree, we're here for your bark. We want to build a canoe. I guess we wanted to thank you for growing so big and strong for us. We're sorry for what this is going to do to you. But it looks like you've lived a long and good life. Long and good." His voice caught in his throat for a moment. "If you let us use your bark to make a canoe, in a way you'll be part of our family forever. We're good people. And we mean well, even if sometimes we fall short."

My mother was crying quietly by the time he finished. Marty and I didn't say anything.

Eugene came around and showed Dad how to make the incision, how to dig the hook of the knife in deep and pull it around the circumference. With the help of a ladder, we did another cut twenty feet up, and then one long zipper-cut from top to bottom. Eugene helped us peel the bark off the tree. It was like removing a stiff jacket from a corpse.

≈

I think we all felt better once we got our rolled-up sheet of bark back to the camp. Big Angus had dug out trenches in the sandy soil, one for each group of canoe-builders.

He showed us how to unroll our bark and weight it down with heavy stones. Slowly, the four of us bent the edges upward and braced it with pine timbers the way Big Angus had showed us. It was hard work. And it really did take a team effort.

"You got that corner, Jeannie?" my dad would ask.

"Check."

"Jack, you go with that piece over there. No, that one. Good. Now, Marty, help him with that clamp the way Big Angus showed us."

We were busy. Occupied. There wasn't time to think about things that had happened or what we could have done to prevent them. There was only the bark and the bending and the work.

By the end of the day, we were sore. Sweat had mixed with dirt and dried, so our skin was covered with a salty grit. But we had something that resembled an actual canoe. If any of us knew how far we still were from the finished product, we probably would have packed up and left after that first day. But we didn't know, couldn't know: To build a thing like this would take a lot more suffering.

≈

That evening, each of the groups claimed their own section of the property to set up camp. Dad wanted to stick close to our canoe-in-progress, but Mom said we needed privacy, so we pitched our tent at the edge of a clearing, as far away from the others as possible.

Dinner was mac and cheese cooked on the camp stove. Afterwards, we wandered over to Big Angus's trailer where a good-sized campfire was blazing. He and Eugene sat on lawn chairs, staring into the flames. The Wetzels were sitting on a log, all of them lined up from biggest to smallest.

We took a spot on a log opposite the Wetzels. My mom and dad sat on either side of Marty and me, which I wasn't fond of since it made me seem younger in front of the Wetzel girls.

"How long have you been in the canoe game, Angus?" Dad asked.

"I'm from the Bear Clan, where most of the best canoe makers come from," he said. "I guess you could say I was born into it."

The fraternity brothers had set up their camp a ways off in the woods. We could hear them cracking beers, and every once in a while they'd break into a chant.

"There's a story we tell in the Bear Clan," Big Angus said. It was hard to be sure in the growing dusk, but it seemed like he was looking at my mother. Not in a lascivious way, more out of what might be concern. "A story that goes back to the olden days. A girl was just reaching the age to find a suitable husband. And this fellow fancied her. But she didn't want nothing to do with him. And it wounded his pride something fierce."

I could sense my mother shifting uneasily on the log next to me.

"It was winter and this fellow went out late one night and took some snow. He crushed it so tight it became the hardest ball of ice you ever seen. And he snuck into the girl's wigwam and placed the ice on the girl's chest."

I heard my mom whisper "Good God" under her breath.

"The next morning, the girl woke up sick. And the next few days she had a terrible temper. She knew she was becoming what some people call a *Chenoo* and some call a *Wintiku*."

"What's that?" the eldest Wetzel girl asked.

"It's a powerful creature," Big Angus said. "Maybe the most powerful. Almost impossible to kill without magic. And they're dangerous too. They have to eat. Always. They'll eat a whole village without even thinking about it." The lenses of his glasses reflected the fire—two orange circles in the middle of his face.

"So this girl knew what she was becoming and knew it would be trouble for her family and everyone she loved. She told the elders to kill her before it was too late. In order to do it right, they had to take the seven bravest warriors of the Bear Clan, and each one had to shoot her with an arrow."

My mother sighed loudly.

"So the first six archers took aim, and their arrows hit the mark. But the last archer was the same fellow who put the ice on the girl's chest in the first place. He couldn't bring himself to kill her, so he missed on purpose."

The Wetzels were bunched close together on their log, the daughters clearly frightened. But Big Angus went on: "The girl began to shake and they knew she was close to turning, so they took her to the river and threw her into the deepest part, and the water froze solid, all the way through." Big Angus looked up from the fire. At first he seemed surprised to see us there, but then he smiled. "That's where she's been ever since," he said. "Whenever spring comes, we make offerings to the river, ask it to hold her until the ice returns."

It was quiet around the fire for a moment.

"That's a shitty story, Angus." My dad's voice caught me by surprise. It was low, and angrier than I'd ever heard it sound before.

"Michael!" Mom said.

"I've got this, Jeannie."

"No, Michael, it's Marty. He's gone!"

It was true. Somehow during the story, Marty had disappeared.

"Goddammit," my dad said, springing from the log.

"Marty!" Mom called out.

We all listened, but there was no answer.

"Okay, Jeannie," my dad said, "you try the tent, I'll check with those frat guys." They both took off in different directions.

I looked around the fire, at the Wetzels and Big Angus and Eugene. Then I decided to check our canoe-in-progress, since that seemed like the kind of place Marty would hide. The path was dark, and I nearly tripped twice on overgrown tree roots. It turned out I was right. My brother was sitting in our canoe, his back stiff, staring straight ahead.

"Hey," I said, but he didn't turn to acknowledge me.

I sat down next to him, outside the canoe, resting my hand on what would eventually become the starboard gunwale.

"Where did you go?" I asked.

"Right here," he said, blinking earnestly.

"Sorry. Stupid question." I could hear agitated voices filtering through the trees, but I couldn't tell what they were saying.

"Why did you wander off?" I asked. "You shouldn't worry Mom like that."

"I didn't like that story," he said. "It reminded me of Collette."

"It's not really the same, Marty." But I knew what I said was false. What happened to our sister would always be at the center of our lives. My family, the four of us now, would be planets forever revolving around that moment. So I said, "I guess everything is always the same."

Marty smiled. I think this made him feel better.

At that moment, a moth fluttered between us, its wings powdery-gray in the moonlight. To both our surprise, it landed on the tip of Marty's nose. But he didn't swat it or shoo it away, as I surely would have done. Instead, he looked at it for a moment, his eyes going slightly cross-eyed, and he said, "This is a job for The Human Hologram."

Then he made a platform of his hand and invited the moth to move onto it. He held the moth out above his head until it thwipped its wings and took flight, in search of light or warmth or whatever moths seek.

"Should we go back to the campfire?" I asked.

"In a minute," Marty said. He was looking up into the sky. "How did the story end?" he asked.

I wondered what to tell him. The answer seemed important, though I'm not sure why. "Those kinds of stories usually end badly," I said. "But they're not like real life. Not always."

Boy in the Bubble

About once a week, on his way home from work, Paul Corbin would turn left onto Peele Street and drive right by his house, the very house his family had been living in for the past five years. It was a mental hiccup that had been going on for a few months. He usually went a block or two before realizing his error, at which point he'd execute a three-point turn and go back down Peele Street at a crawl, searching desperately for a landmark.

Initially he'd worried this was a harbinger of senility. But thirty-six, he figured, was still a bit early. And he'd experienced no similar stiffening of his mental agility at work; if anything, things had been going better than usual there. So Paul was forced to look elsewhere for an explanation.

"We're missing another wine glass."

Paul looked up from the soapy sink. His hands were warm and pink like a newborn's.

"That's the second glass in a week." His wife's hair was tousled in a careless way that never failed to faintly arouse him. "Maybe you've been breaking them and not telling me."

Paul wrung the sponge out and set it on the edge of the sink. "Maybe you've been secretly having an affair and your lover is a butterfingers."

Trina's face went slack, giving her a jowly look. It was true that Paul's sense of humor had been off by a few degrees lately. But he wondered if there had been a time, once, when Trina would have found at least a shred of something funny in what he'd just said.

"I'm sorry," he said. "Stupid joke."

She dried a plate with the dishtowel until it made angry squeaking noises.

In moments like these, he wished he had the strength to take her in his arms and squeeze her until whatever barriers had been erected between them crumbled. But he knew these kinds of walls did not surrender to brute force. Nor did they yield to attrition. They were built strong—piece upon interlocking piece—and they were, as far as he knew, indestructible.

Through the window above the sink, his eye caught the tent in the backyard, glowing with the light of a fluorescent Coleman lantern. Trina noticed his stare and followed it.

"Do you think we should be letting him camp out in the backyard like that?"

"He's safe, Trina. We chose this neighborhood so he could do exactly this kind of thing."

She huffed upwards and her breath fluttered her bangs. "It's not his safety that concerns me, Paul."

"Then what? Are you worried the tent's gonna damage the grass?" Paul groped around in the soapy water for stray pieces of silverware. "Because I guarantee there'll be a dead patch. That's something I've already come to terms with."

"I'm not joking," she said. "I don't think it's normal for a ten-year-old boy to want to spend the entire summer camping in the backyard."

Paul had already considered this. Two weeks ago, when Max announced his decision, it had struck Paul as a tad antisocial. But he couldn't tell if it fell within the bell curve of normal. What truly concerned him, though, was what would happen when the weather turned cold and Max was forced to fold up the tent and move back inside. Would he be the same boy he was at the beginning of the summer? Or would he be the kind of kid who wore camouflage, wrote nasty plans in a secret notebook, dreamed of torturing animals? These were the questions that made the skin on Paul's scalp go tight.

"Cub Scouts didn't work out, Trina. I think it's okay to let him indulge his inner mountain man."

She shook her head. "Did you ever consider why Cub Scouts didn't work out?" There was an exhaustion in his wife's voice, but Paul couldn't tell who it was directed toward.

"He's a good kid. He's just—" Paul felt a sharp bite against the pad of his thumb. A rose-tinted cloud formed in the dishwater.

"What is it?"

Paul cradled his thumb and held it to his chest. "A knife!" he shouted. "There's a knife in the sink." With the pain came a sharp edge of accusation.

"Let me see it."

"Did you leave a knife in there?" This kind of carelessness was just like Trina, he thought. "Did you?"

"Quit whining and let me take a look."

Paul offered his thumb to her the way you'd hand someone a dirty tissue. Her hands felt rough on his water-softened skin.

"Does that hurt?" she asked.

"Ow!"

"Hang on." She dropped his hand and started for the bathroom. "Let me get the peroxide."

"You were supposed to find a repairman for the dishwasher last week," he called out to her, but she either didn't hear or chose not to respond. Paul put his thumb in his mouth and sucked at the seeping blood.

≈

"Are you sure you don't want to sleep inside tonight, buddy?" Paul's head brushed against the roof of the tent as he sat cross-legged near the zippered opening.

"What happened to your thumb?" Max asked.

Paul instinctively tucked his bandaged thumb in his fist. "Nothing. I cut it washing the dishes."

"You should be more careful, Dad."

"Maybe you could help your old man out and do the dishes every once in a while."

Nothing from Max, not even a smile. Max had thick black hair, like Trina's. His eyes were set far apart and they were unreadable.

"What if it rains?" Paul asked.

"It hasn't rained in, like, twenty-three days." Max pointed to the shortwave radio, which he'd set up on an old army footlocker. "Besides, on the news they said there's maybe a five percent chance of showers tonight and tomorrow."

Paul put his hands up in defense. "Hey, it's not me that's worried, buddy. It's your mom. You know how she is."

"No, I don't," Max said studiously. "How *is* she?"

Max reminded Paul of those pre-Renaissance paintings where they hadn't yet learned how to make the baby Jesus look like a real child and instead he always came out looking like a miniature adult, a precocious wise-man-in-the-making.

Once, when Max was eight, Paul had taken him to Baskin-Robbins after a soccer game. The boy behind the counter had stared rudely at Max as he'd taken their order. Later, when they were walking out to the car, Paul had overheard the Baskin-Robbins kid talking to a coworker.

"Did you see that boy in the soccer uniform?" Baskin-Robbins had asked his coworker; the two of them were huddled together next to the dumpster, sneaking a cigarette, oblivious.

His coworker was a skinny girl with streaks of blue in her hair. "Nah," she'd said. "Why?"

"I don't know, man. He was creepy. Like Damien. Or that kid in *Problem Child*."

"I love that movie!" the girl said, and they'd both laughed like this was the funniest thing they'd heard in weeks.

Paul had glared at the clueless coworkers, wishing hateful things on the guy, fantasizing about causing actual, physical harm. But he'd just steered Max into the car, slamming the door loudly enough to get their attention at last, meanwhile praying that his son hadn't heard the exchange.

And now in the tent, Paul felt the closeness of the air, and realized he was sweating. "So you're not coming in, then."

"That's right," Max said, unrolling his sleeping bag. The bag was olive green, lined with flannel that had pictures of wood ducks floating on a serene lake.

"Doesn't it get boring out here?" He was stalling, and he suspected Max knew it.

"I manage to keep myself occupied." Max gestured vaguely at the radio and a stack of library books near the footlocker.

"What are you reading?"

"Lately I've been checking out this book on the Native Americans who used to live around these parts. I'm reading the chapter on social customs right now." Max's eyebrows flexed. "Did you know that when boys reached a certain age they had to leave their tribes to go on these vision quests?"

Paul nodded dutifully.

"They had to wander around alone in the forests for, like, months or something."

"Sounds scary."

Max bit his lip in thought. "Not really," he said. "What would happen is they were supposed to see this animal that would tell them what to do. What kind of person they were supposed to be."

"Pretty heavy stuff." Paul was always a little surprised when he heard himself having actual conversations with his son.

"Yeah. Sometimes these kids would go crazy and die. Or sometimes they'd just never come back."

"Do you believe in that stuff?"

Max scrutinized his father for a moment. "If you mean do I believe people went on vision quests, then yes. But if you mean do I believe they actually talked with animals, then I don't know, Dad. Maybe some of them did."

Paul was wary of the topic now and decided to change tacks. "Don't you get scared being out here by yourself?"

Max gazed steadily at his father. Paul thought he might see a spark in his eyes, some kind of mirthful intelligence at work.

"There's plenty of things I'm scared of, Dad. Being alone is not one of them."

A cushion of silence expanded and filled the dome tent. Paul searched for the right words to prick and deflate it, but could not find them. His eyes wandered over to Max's walkie-talkie, which was hanging in a mesh side pocket. Paul plucked it out and turned it over in his hands. It was rounded and yellow and plastic, with a short rubber antennae. He clicked the device on and put it back. "I've got mine right next to me in bed, buddy. Any problems, just say the word and I'll be out here in a jiff."

Max climbed into his sleeping bag and nodded, but didn't say anything.

≈

Inside, Paul stood at the kitchen sink, staring out the window at the glowing dome in the backyard. He fingered the bandage on his cut thumb. He pressed it against a knuckle, feeling reassurance at the pain it produced, as if the ache might make him a more solid person, might keep him from dissolving before his own eyes.

The tinny sounds of an old sitcom drifted in from the living room. The laugh track sounded exaggerated and inappropriate.

A year ago, Trina had gotten a severe case of the flu, from which it had taken her three months to fully recover. During her convalescence, she'd developed a sudden and insatiable appetite for TV sitcoms, to the exclusion of all else. Paul had grown so tired of the forced cheeriness that he'd eventually had to stop watching. Now it was something Trina did alone. She'd watch until she fell asleep on the couch, and the TV would hum all night long, bathing the living room in a cold blue light.

The sickness had forced her to take a leave of absence from teaching. She hadn't gone back, though she occasionally mentioned it as something she'd like to do when things normalized. That was her word: *normalized.* As if this was somehow not normal—as if this, right here, was not what their lives had become.

Eventually, the lantern in the tent switched off, and the backyard sank into a gloomy darkness. The tent was visible only as a vague cloudlike shape near the ground.

≈

Paul turned the dial on his walkie-talkie, setting the volume somewhere in the middle. The initial staticky hiss of the receiver ebbed into a soothing white noise. The walkie-talkies had a hands-free setting, so they triggered automatically when a sound was sufficiently loud.

"Good night, Max," Paul intoned quietly, hoping he wasn't disturbing his son.

Paul heard the sound of a heavy sigh, the rustlings of a person turning over.

"Dad," said the voice over the speaker, "if you ever had another baby with someone who wasn't Mom, would you name him Max like me?"

Paul lay in bed, pinned and sweating against the mattress. "There's only one Max, buddy."

"No there's not," his son said. His voice had a dreamy quality to it, as if he might be talking in his sleep. "There's two Maxes in the fourth grade." And then his breathing slowed into a steady rhythm, and Paul listened until he was quite sure his son was asleep.

≈

Paul was putting the finishing touches on a presentation for a proposed sewer project when his desk phone rang.

"Paul, there's something wrong out here." It was Trina. He detected a note of alarm in her voice.

"What is it?"

"I was out in Max's tent this afternoon while he was at his piano lesson. I was just straightening up, you know. I wasn't trying to snoop or anything…"

"What happened?"

"A bottle of wine, Paul. He had a bottle of wine in his footlocker. One of our Louis Bernards."

"He stole a bottle of wine?" Paul was unable to square the details of the crime with his image of Max.

"Why do you think he'd do that, Paul?" She sounded genuinely concerned, which secretly pleased him. It momentarily trumped the fact that his own son was possibly on the road to becoming someone he might not like.

"What did you do with the bottle, Trina?" This seemed important to Paul. He didn't know why.

"Nothing," she said defensively. "I left it there." The line went silent for a moment. Then: "What should we do?"

"Maybe you should talk to him, Trina."

"Well, I… I don't know what I'd say." Paul could sense a retreat in her voice.

"Why don't you just tell him the first thing that pops into your head," he said, a little sadistically.

"Paul, you're better at this kind of thing than me."

"I guess I could talk to him," he said. "If you prefer. When I get home from work."

"Good," she said, a bit too quickly. "I think this is the kind of thing a father should handle."

≈

"Do you want to tell me why you did this?"

"Not really." Max was staring at the floor of the tent. The bottle of wine rested on its side between them, unopened.

Paul had missed the house on the way home from work again. That made twice in one week—which was a new and troubling record. The implications of this were weighing on his mind as he sat in the nylon dome.

"Were you going to drink it?" he asked.

"I don't know." There was a gruff edge to his son's voice, the first intonations of teenage resentment.

"Have you ever drunk alcohol before, Max?"

"No, Dad."

"I don't want you lying to me." The air in the tent was warm and sticky. Paul could feel his shirt clinging to his armpits.

"I'm not lying! Sheesh."

"Don't *sheesh* me! Your mother and I are very concerned about this."

The fact was, they'd never had to punish Max before. He got good grades, did what he was told. If anything, he was a little *too* good. Paul wouldn't have minded if Max had gotten into trouble for any of the minor infractions a kid his age was supposed to commit, like talking back to a teacher or playing Ding-Dong-Ditch with the neighborhood kids. Those were understandable, even acceptable, if kept within certain limits.

"Is there anything wrong, buddy? With your friends?" Paul knew Max was the sort of kid who might have problems with bullies. He was small for his age and he had the kind of sensibility that encouraged taunting from those who preyed on the weak. Paul had enrolled Max in karate classes, but he'd quit after two sessions, complaining that he couldn't stand all the yelling, and that the dojo smelled like dirty feet.

"I hope you know you can tell me anything, Max. I'm your father, but I'm also your friend, right?"

"Sure, Dad," he chirped.

Paul couldn't tell if there was a note of sarcasm buried in his son's tone.

"This has got to stop," Paul said at last. "No more of this...this business." He took the wine bottle by the throat. "Understood?"

"I understand." His eyes were still fixed on the floor.

"Okay, then." Paul shifted his weight, getting ready to leave. "I'm going to see if your mom needs help with dinner."

"Dad?" Now Max's eyebrows were low with concern. "What's wrong with Mom?"

Paul felt something churn inside him, a deep unsettling of the intestines. He recognized this moment for what it was: the kind of scene that would lodge in his child's brain and be remembered forever. And he had no script for this, no idea what the next line should be.

"You mean like why isn't she working right now, Max?"

Max fiddled with the zipper on his sleeping bag. "I guess I'm talking about something different," he said. "Like why is she so sad?"

A gust of breath rushed up from Paul's lungs, and it came out sounding like a sob. "I don't know, son. She was very sick a while back. That was a hard thing for her."

Max nodded. He seemed lost in contemplation. Paul wished he could view his son's thoughts, put whatever fears he had to rest. That seemed like the least a father could do for his son.

"Do you think she's lonely?"

Paul braced his hand against the cold ground to steady himself. "Yes, Max, I do."

"I figured." Max stood up and moved to the radio at the back of the tent. He started twisting the dial. "Are you lonely, Dad?"

"Why do you ask?"

"I don't know," Max said. "Sometimes I think it's like a cold or something. Like if a lonely person sneezes, other people might catch it too."

"Are you lonely, son?"

Max looked up at him. His hair was statically charged from rubbing against the roof of the tent. "I asked you first, Dad."

"Yes, buddy. I get that way sometimes. But these things go in phases. They don't last forever."

Max frowned for a moment. "I think you're right. I think I might feel that way sometimes too."

"Why don't you move back inside with us? Your bed is waiting for you."

Max turned the radio on, and a low whistling static filled the tent. "I'll move back sometime. But not yet, Dad."

When Paul left the tent, he was unsure if he'd passed this parental test, if he'd been the father his son needed. Maybe it was a moment Max would harbor against him—the time he learned that everyone in the world, sometime or another, is lonely. And all you can do to fight it is hope it eventually goes away.

≈

"What did he say?"

"Not much, Trina."

"What do you mean, *not much*? Did he say why he stole a bottle of his parents' wine?" She was standing at the stove, turning a skillet of snap peas and peppers. Her hair was up and she smelled like lavender bath soap. She was wearing a red bathrobe that hung loosely at her shoulders. Paul caught himself wondering if she was wearing anything underneath.

"I don't think he meant to drink it. He was probably just acting out or something. Kids do silly stuff from time to time. Even our kid."

Paul opened the cabinet and replaced the bottle. He tried to remember how many they'd had before, and if any others were missing. But drinking wine was not something he and Trina did anymore. It was a habit they'd fallen out of—or a rut they'd gotten into, depending on one's point of view.

"I might understand if he were doing this with someone else," Trina said. "But he's doing this on his own. Doesn't that trouble you?"

"Of course it does!" Paul was suddenly angry. "It bothers me that he's alone out there, and it bothers me that you're alone in here."

Trina turned to look at him. The vegetables popped and sizzled in the skillet.

"Whoa," she said. "Where did that come from?"

"Nowhere," Paul said. "I just think he might be a little sad."

"Did he say he was sad?"

"Not exactly. It's something I maybe picked up on." Paul was cautious now. If he wasn't careful here, Max would end up getting weekly sessions with some probing psychologist—which seemed like a cruel precaution at this point.

"It's just a rebellious phase, Trina. We should be happy. Most kids start selling meth and getting girls pregnant in their rebellious phases. Sneaking a bottle of wine is lightweight by comparison."

She took the skillet off the burner and balanced the spatula on the edge. "I just hope that...with everything, you know, how things haven't really normalized around here."

The sound of that word—normalized—riggered something in Paul. "Everything is normal here!" His voice spiked. "Everything is normal."

She looked at him, incredulous. "You really don't understand a thing, do you, Paul? Not one goddamn thing."

≈

That night, after Max had retired to his tent and Trina to the living room couch, Paul tossed in bed, unable to sleep.

Max had been sullen at dinner, staring at his food, saying little. Trina had been equally downcast. Paul tried to talk about his presentation for the sewer proposal, explaining how it would help improve drainage at several major intersections downtown. The presentation had been a coup, winning unanimous support from the city planning council. But Trina and Max were uninterested. Paul felt like a man with one foot on a pier and the other on an unmoored boat that was drifting out to sea.

The sounds of Max sleeping came in over the walkie-talkie, mingling with the sounds of his wife's sitcoms in the living room.

Paul ventured an arm across the wide acreage of the bed. The sheets felt smooth and cool and empty. Something other than his wife, it seemed, was missing. A pillow, maybe. He felt around with his hand. There was definitely an absence, an asymmetry, but Paul couldn't be sure what it was.

≈

"Do you want to tell me why you did this?"

Paul was sitting in the tent. Max was leafing through a library book. A curtain of black bangs hung over his eyes. Trina had called Paul at work. A week ago she'd discovered the wine in the footlocker; today she'd found a padlock on the footlocker.

"It's no big deal, Dad. I just wanted some privacy. I used to use this lock for my bicycle, but I wasn't using it anymore."

Paul had missed the house on the way home from work again, and the experience had left him reeling. It was as if, by turning onto Peele Street, his mind entered some foggy region, and he was unable to see or think clearly.

"I want to know why you think you need privacy, young man." Paul tried to find the right parental tone with his voice. "What is so important that you have to lock your things up?"

"I have some pretty valuable comics, dad. Some of them could be worth a lot of money someday."

"Is that all you have in there?"

Max looked up from his book and blinked, as if he were unused to such bright light. "Of course I have some other stuff in there," he said. "But it's personal."

"You're ten years old. What do you have that's personal?"

Max seemed oddly unflustered by this exchange; he had a peaceful, almost serene look on his face.

"Do you have anything you keep secret, Dad? From Mom and me?" Max's dark eyes were riveted on Paul. They seemed to be prying at him, needling.

"Yes, son," Paul said. "I do. But they're not bad things. They're nothing I'm ashamed of."

Max smiled. "That's how I feel about my footlocker. If you want I can give you the combination. Do you want that, Dad?"

"Sure, buddy. I'd like that very much."

Max looked at the palm of his hand where he'd written a series of numbers in blue ballpoint pen. "It's 26-34-12." He said the numbers quietly, in a low voice, like a priest bestowing a blessing.

Paul silently committed the numbers to memory.

"Do you want to look in my footlocker, Dad? I don't mind."

Paul turned the question over in his mind. This was a test.

"No, Max. As long as you don't have anything in there you shouldn't have, I don't need to look."

Max set the book aside and smiled brightly. "I'm glad we had this talk," he said.

"So am I."

"Did you know, Dad, that this one Indian brave went on a vision quest, but instead of finding a spirit animal, he found a spirit snowstorm. He said the snowstorm talked to him. When he came back to the tribe they named him Walks Through Ice."

When Paul failed to say anything, Max shrugged. "I guess I just thought that was pretty cool. You know."

Paul, to his surprise, agreed.

≈

"Do you realize how naïve you're being?" Trina stood in the doorway between the kitchen and the living room, prepared at any moment to slip off into her world of sitcoms, her private bubble of fake laughter.

"It's a question of trust," he said.

"Christ, Paul, why can't you see it? Your child is slipping away."

"My child? *My* child!" He couldn't help the raised voice.

Trina took a step back. The darkness of the living room fell across her face. The sudden shift in light made her seem farther away than she really was.

"I wish you wouldn't just roll over when you should be calling him out on this kind of thing, Paul."

He glanced out the kitchen window at the glowing tent. He thought he saw movement through the thin nylon fabric, and he wondered briefly what Max might be doing in there.

"I'm not rolling over," he said. "I'm giving him space." He thought about Walks Through Ice talking to the howling raging winds of a snowstorm. "And besides, if anyone around here has rolled over, it sure as hell isn't me."

Her chin tilted down slightly. "You don't have to be so cheap."

"Just out of curiosity," he said, shifting his weight. "When was the last time you actually had a conversation with your son?"

She shook her head. "Don't think you're any more present than I am, just because you do more talking."

"What's that supposed to mean?"

Her shoulders shuddered and then the air seemed to leak from her lungs. "This is not working out," she hissed, the words barely audible. She took a step back, then another, until she was lost completely to the darkness of the living room.

≈

It was some time late that night when Paul awoke to the grainy crackle of his son's voice over the walkie-talkie.

"Dad!" There was an urgency in Max's voice which rattled Paul from his sleep. "Dad, help, come out here, quick!"

It was the one thing he'd most feared hearing since Max moved outside. Before he could open his eyes, Paul was pierced with a thought: he'd spent his whole life idly drifting, waiting for the worst things to happen, without ever taking the right steps to prevent them from happening. And this, right now, was the result.

He shot out of bed and scrambled for the door. His heart pressed against his ribcage like an overinflated balloon. Moving through the dark, Paul stumbled on a pile of dirty laundry. He felt his balance go as he sprawled headlong and crashed into the thick carpet. He felt the skin on his elbows burn and he let out a yelp.

"What is it?" Trina's voice from the living room. "Paul, what—"

"Max," was all he could manage as he struggled to his feet and raced to the back door.

The grass in the backyard had already gathered a coat of dew and it felt cool on Paul's bare feet. The lantern in the tent was on and Paul sprinted toward it.

He reached the tent and lifted the flap. It took Paul several seconds to take in what he saw.

On the footlocker was an open bottle of red wine. Next to the bottle were two wine glasses, half full. The shortwave radio played a slow jazz song, and a woman's low sultry voice sang something about love.

"What is it, Paul?" Trina's voice was frantic. She nudged him aside so she could peer into the tent.

"Max?" Paul called out, though his son was obviously not there.

The flimsy speaker of the walkie-talkie crackled.

"Mom, Dad, I want you to know that, effective tonight, I've decided to move back into the house."

"Where are you, Max? Honey?"

"Don't worry, Mom." Max's voice was calm. "Tomorrow we can take the tent down. In the meantime, maybe you'd like to see what it's like to sleep out there."

Paul noticed that the floor of the tent was covered with white downy fluff. He picked up a handful and realized it was feathers. "Our pillow," he said quietly.

"I'm going to turn off the walkie-talkie now, you guys. I just wanted to wish you goodnight."

There was a slight click and the speaker went silent. The song on the radio ended and another began and Paul looked at Trina. She was wearing a long white t-shirt that stopped a third of the way down her thighs. She crawled into the tent. Paul followed her. The walls felt close around them. Trina picked up a scoop of white feathers and tossed them overhead. They fluttered about the tent, like a snow globe that had just been given a good hard shake.

Paul picked up a wine glass. The wine shimmered a deep burgundy. "I guess this is for us," he said.

He handed the glass to Trina. "For us," she said.

As a cool breeze ruffled the tent flaps outside, Paul thought about vision quests: boys on the cusp of adulthood who'd been given glimpses of their own destinies. And then he thought about how no matter what that vision was—good or bad, life-changing or inconsequential—they all had to face, when it was over, the long walk back to the tribe.

Stormy Night

Our apartment building doesn't have central air, so the upstairs neighbors' fights are worse when it's hot, like tonight. This one starts around nine when he gets home late, again.

Beforehand, Chloe and I are sitting in the living room reading, waiting. We haven't spoken in thirty minutes. We are trying our best to ignore the heat. I glance over the edge of my magazine, not sure if I expect her to be crying or fuming. She looks at her watch and casts her eyes toward the ceiling.

A few moments later we hear a key fumbling at the door. "Here he comes," Chloe says.

"And there they go," I add, as the first notes of outrage descend through the paper-thin floors.

Since we moved in, Chloe and I have been privy to every word of their frequent and heated arguments. Gradually, we made a hobby out of it. We're like sportscasters calling Game 7. We dissect and analyze each spat with microscopic scrutiny, categorize each squabble on the basis of length, intensity, and subject matter. We used to talk about getting a TV or even moving, but it's been months since either of us brought it up.

"She was expecting you for dinner two hours ago," Chloe says.

"Tell her that big meeting went long," I say. "The one with the Armenians."

"Such a liar," Chloe says, and shoots me a hard glance.

I'm not trying to be an apologist for the guy. I just wish he'd defend himself once in a while. He lets her tear into him. Sometimes I need to protect him from Chloe too.

The guy is trying to explain why he's late, but not doing a good job. He's talking too loudly, slurring his words. Chloe seizes on this.

"He's been drinking. Call him on it, lady. Don't be such a weakling."

We know their names—Trent and Judy Norwood. We've passed them in the hallway numerous times, but as we sit in our apartment listening, we choose to ignore the actual details of their lives. Instead, we breathe our own life into them, create a couple in our own image.

"He's out getting drunk with some bitch from the office while you're at home with an empty bed." Chloe folds her arms like she's made an indisputable point.

"It's typical for Armenians to celebrate closing a big deal with a toast," I say. "To not share a drink would've been an insult to their culture."

"He needs to be home more," Chloe says. "He's got to be a *full-time partner*." She speaks these last words slowly, as if I'm supposed to find a special meaning in them.

"How can he be at home more when he's the only one *bringing home a paycheck*?" I mimic the tone she just took with me.

As soon as the words are out of my mouth, I regret it. Chloe is between jobs right now, temping at a local radio station.

"Nice," she says. "Really nice." Her voice is trembling. "Like you have any idea what that woman's going through." She picks up the book she's been reading and buries her nose in it.

It's safe to say we are experts on our neighbors' lives. Here are some facts we know:

1. They've been married for twenty-one months.

2. They've been unhappy for most of that time.

3. She can be an incredible nag because she blames him for things he can't control.

4. He can be calculatingly mean and dismissive with only a few words.

5. They both fear saying how they really feel, the things lurking behind the petty arguments.

Basically, they are a typical couple with an average amount of garden-variety shortcomings. They could be anyone, given the right circumstances. Maybe that's what we find so fascinating about them.

Upstairs they're sulking now. She's left the kitchen; he's eating his dinner standing over the sink. That's probably for the best right now. It's sweltering out tonight, and not getting any cooler. The little window A/C units we're allowed to have aren't doing shit. It's been like this all week. The fighting's been bad too. Mean, ugly stuff. I haven't told Chloe, but I'm getting worried about them. If this keeps up, I don't see how they'll last much longer. That would be devastating for us. We've invested so much time and energy into this relationship.

"Looks like they're taking a break," I say, to make conversation. "Good move. Take a little time to cool off."

Chloe bristles. "It'll take more than a time-out. What about the affair?" Her words linger between us for a moment.

Chloe first told me she suspected infidelity six weeks ago. I've been denying it, though I'm as certain as she, and I've known it longer. The signs were obvious: staying later at work without explanation; taking showers immediately after getting home; absorbing himself for hours on end in meaningless tasks, like fixing an uneven stool, or re-attaching a piece of carpet fringe. His mind never seems to be engaged with anything having to do with her anymore.

Every time Chloe mentions infidelity, I break into a sweat, and my face goes pale. I have no excuse for the guy. She's glaring at me now, waiting. It's a test. My response is going to be important, I can tell.

"I don't know where you're getting this idea about an affair," I say in a calm, careful voice. "You have no proof."

"Why can't you just admit it?" Chloe slams her book on the coffee table and stomps into the bedroom. She flops down on the bed and doesn't say a word, but I know she's still listening. The acoustics are just as good in the bedroom.

I imagine it's not the healthiest thing in the world, living so much of our lives through another couple, especially one with so many problems. But neither of us can stop. It's too strong a habit. After a while, you forget how to talk about anything else.

Chloe is quiet in the bedroom now. I look at the clock and see it's almost midnight. Heat lightning flashes on the horizon. All week the forecast has been saying thunderstorms, and all week it's been wrong. I pray for rain, hoping a cool breeze and the comforting smell of drops on the sidewalk outside will soothe these open wounds. I am answered only by a blast of the same oppressive air that's enveloped us for days, and another distant flash of lightning.

I go to the bedroom, strip down to my boxers, slip quietly into bed. I stare at the ceiling, listening to our neighbors get closer to the breaking point. They're not fighting about his late arrival anymore. It's evolved into something more elemental, the root of their unhappiness.

This type of argument is the most dangerous kind. It's so easy for one person to screw up and say they're sick of the other person, that they wish they'd never married, that they never should have been together in the first place. I have a feeling this might be a night when lines are crossed. I am on edge.

One of them drops something heavy on the floor and I flinch.

"Stormy night," Chloe whispers. I had been hoping she was asleep.

"No, honey," I whisper back, thinking maybe she's dreaming or asking about the weather.

"I mean upstairs." She holds her breath for a moment and listens. "Such an asshole," she says, just as I reach out to touch her ribs.

Her body is tight, like an over-wound spring. The raised voices have gotten to her. Too much fighting. Too much anger. Too much hiding below the surface. Things can't go on this way. Any minute someone's going to lash out. My ears are pricked, waiting to hear a slap or a punch or something being thrown across the room, the sound of pain.

I can hardly breathe. I'm desperate. I lean over and kiss Chloe on the neck, hoping for more, thinking it might somehow help counter the rancor drifting down from upstairs. She pulls away and clucks her throat. "I can't right now," she says. "I just can't."

She gets up and goes to the bathroom to fill the glass of water she keeps by the bed. She lets the tap run and run, waiting for the water to turn cold.

I roll back onto my side of the bed. The worn-out mattress absorbs me. I put a pillow over my ears and it blots out all the noise—the fighting upstairs, the raging faucet in our bathroom. It is as quiet as the empty promise of the heat lightning. Isolated and alone, I hunker down and let myself sink in deeper.

Chloe comes out of the bathroom leaving the light on. She is a silhouette in the doorway, a wraith. I sit up suddenly, the pillow falling off my ears.

It is, for the first time tonight, silent upstairs.

"It's over," she says. And I'm not sure who she's talking about.

Coyote in the City

Ellis Jackson knew he'd taken the easiest route life had offered. Coming out of high school, he'd gotten a football scholarship to a Division II school, but he opted instead to stay in Billings and follow his father into the roofing business. The job suited him. It was outdoors and it engaged his senses—the sticky tar vapors, the rough feel of new shingles, the satisfying kick of the nailgun as it snicked another nail home. The work was a language he understood, a mantra chanted in his native tongue.

After a brief apprenticeship, he started his own roofing company. And he started a family that same year. For the next decade, both of them happily grew. But he knew his decisions had left him vulnerable, and this knowledge stuck with him the way a page in a book, once dog-eared, never looks quite like the others again.

A prolonged slump in the housing market caused work orders to nosedive. Within two years, he had to sell off the company truck, and then the roofing equipment. He was forced to go on public assistance to feed his wife and three young sons. The nightly news often ran stories talking of others in situations similar to his, but he didn't know those people. They seemed distant and foreign to him.

Relief came that spring in the form of a job with the Billings City Parks Department. It was seasonal work—lasting only the summer—and the pay was brutally low. He was thirty-one, emptying garbage in his hometown, a city whose orbit he'd never seriously thought about leaving.

≈

It didn't take Jackson long to adjust to the contours of the job. Every day he drove around Billings alone in a Ford F-350 modified to hold a dumpster and hydraulic brusher on the back. He had free rein to go wherever he wanted—no accountability except to the garbage itself, and to the occasional call from his boss Kent on the truck's CB.

In the mornings, Jackson would rush through the garbage pick-up at the bigger parks in the heart of the city, then take his time at the smaller ones out west in the afternoons. It was here that he was least likely to encounter people he knew, least likely to see that slight downward cast in their eyes when they saw his green parks t-shirt.

Often, as he drove through these freshly built neighborhoods, Jackson would remind himself that he'd personally roofed a good number of these houses. Then a moment later he'd catch a whiff of the trash he was hauling, and his stomach would clench at the thought of what he'd do for a job when the summer was over.

Every morning before he set off on his route, he pored over the meager job listings in the classifieds. Afterwards, if there was time, he'd turn to the local section. One morning in early June he came across an article that caught his attention.

The previous day there had been mountain lion sightings around the commercial big-box strip west of town. Animal control officers cornered the mountain lion in the loading dock behind a Lowe's. They tranquilized the creature, tagged it, and relocated it further outside the city. But they warned that if it turned up again inside the city limits, they'd have to euthanize it. The story made Jackson quake with a slow, boiling rage. He fought the urge to crumple the newspaper into a ball.

In mid-July he came across another article. This time a juvenile coyote, maybe one or two years old, came in off the prairies and wandered down 24th Street on the west end until it found a Quiznos with the front door propped open. It scurried inside, jumped up on the counter, surveyed the employees and the handful of people eating a late lunch, then proceeded to take a seat on the glass lid of a cooler. Again, animal control was summoned. Because coyotes enjoyed no federal or state protections, it was put down.

Jackson wondered why this was happening. Were these animals somehow pulled in to the city? Or was the city pushing out toward them? He tore the newspaper into scraps and flung them out the truck window. Then, worried someone might see the city logo on the door and report him, he climbed out of the truck and picked them up. He tossed them into the rear bin, then worked the sweep-and-slide levers, to push the torn paper into the bottom of the dumpster.

One afternoon in early August he pulled his truck up to the first set of cans at Forest Glen Park. His eyes traced the perimeter of the green square. There was a set of netless basketball hoops on one end, an abandoned playground on the other. Then he saw the trees.

"Hey, Kent," he said into the CB mouthpiece. "Are you there?"

The speaker cracked and whistled. "That's not proper CB protocol, Jackson."

"Kent, I'm at Forest Glen. You need to get out here and see this."

"See what?"

Every tree in the park—numbering probably two dozen—had been cut down at roughly eight feet high. Next to the tall stumps, the leafy tops of the trees lay like severed heads.

≈

After the police finished questioning him, Kent ambled over. He was wearing tight jeans and a pearl snap-button shirt, as if he'd just stepped off the pro rodeo circuit.

"That's a hell of a thing, eh?" Kent said.

Jackson watched as a truck drove through the park to dispose of the treetops. Ten years ago, he thought, this was probably farmland. A hundred years ago, it might have been a forest. "Crazy world," he said.

He was about to climb into the truck and resume his collection route when Kent sighed and blew his lips out in a raspberry. "This sure is some kind of a thing."

"Idiot high schoolers maybe," Jackson offered, grateful for the fact that his own sons were not yet that age.

Kent shook his head. He looked at Jackson, eyes squinting in the sun. "You got company tomorrow."

"Company?"

"Yep." He ran his index finger over the thin blond mustache on his lip. "*Uno compañero.*"

"Is it because of these trees?" Jackson tried not to sound bothered, but the fact that he got to work alone was the only good part of the job.

Kent scrunched his face up as if he'd been hurt. "I have an extra man for the time being, and you're the best one to stick him with." He rested a hand on Jackson's shoulder, a gesture that felt too familiar. "This'll be a slick deal. You sit back and drive while this new fella throws the trash in back."

"Really, Kent, I don't need—"

"You get to drive because this guy doesn't have a license." Kent seemed absorbed in his own private giddiness. "On account of he just got out of jail. He's a *parolee*." Kent pressed his tongue against his cheek as if he enjoyed some special taste the word left in his mouth.

≈

The city parks vehicle depot was a fenced-off lot south of town, in an area dotted with corrugated aluminum warehouses and nameless truck repair shops. The trailer that served as the break room was cramped, with a long table and foldout chairs. When Jackson showed up the next morning, Tony Patterson and Freddie Yellow Fox were eating doughnuts and flipping through ancient copies of *Car & Driver*. Neither Tony nor Freddie spoke much to Jackson. They were older—both of them lifers in the parks department. Jackson wasn't sure what they did in the off-season.

He took a seat and began scanning his copy of the *Gazette*.

"Heard you found them trees cut down," Freddie said, leaning back in his chair. "Eight feet high?"

"Sure did," Jackson said, trying to focus on the paper.

"Any idea who did it?"

"Tall people."

Tony found this funny, but Freddie mumbled something that sounded vaguely menacing as he tilted his chair forward and flipped a page in his magazine.

"So were any of you Nancies planning to work for me today?" Kent's sudden appearance in the doorway put a halt to the commotion. "Or did you think I was going to pay you to sit around here punching your puds?"

The men looked sullenly at their boss.

"My partner hasn't shown up yet," Jackson said. "You want me to go out on my own?"

"Sure he has," Kent said. "He's out front waiting on you. He doesn't like confined spaces."

≈

The pale, skinny man leaning against the chain link fence did not fit the profile Jackson had imagined. The guy had sloped shoulders, ropy arms, and a weak chin that made him seem vaguely Muppet-like. He introduced himself as Dean Travers.

"Jackson. I guess we're partners." As they shook hands, Jackson thought: I could take this guy. Not that he wanted, or even expected to, but he knew he could impose his will on this man, if need be.

They climbed into the cab of the truck. "Mind if I smoke?" Dean asked.

"Try and blow it outside." Jackson rolled his own window down, even though the morning air was still cold.

Dean pulled out a dark brown cigarette, some foreign brand Jackson wasn't familiar with, and lit it. Something about Dean's face looked tough—flattened and beaten like a gray cube steak—which made Jackson reconsider his earlier impressions.

Dean was done with his cigarette by the time Jackson eased the truck through the access gate at Pioneer Park. It was the busiest park in the city and Jackson liked to hit it before the crowds of screaming kids and fat picnickers made driving impossible. He pulled the truck to a halt at the first set of garbage cans and looked over at his new partner. Dean stared back through the scratched lenses of his glasses.

This is a moment when dominance will be established, Jackson recognized. What happens now will lay the groundwork for the rest of the day. He flexed his fingers and curled them around the steering wheel as if to dig himself in. "The garbage isn't going to empty itself," he said.

Dean's shoulders were the first thing to cave. Next his gaze lowered, and finally he climbed down from the truck. Jackson watched through the side-view mirror as Dean wrestled with the metal cans. He heard the discordant wake-up call of smashing glass. Then he saw Dean tinkering with the hydraulic levers in back, trying to figure out which one scooped the trash into the tank.

Metal scraping metal: glass ground into dust. Jackson felt a strange elation.

≈

"Holy Christ," Dean said when he climbed back into the truck a few stops later. He was wiping his hands on his jeans. "Looks like someone puked in one of those cans."

"Someone probably did."

Dean sniffed his bare fingers. He winced and made a gagging sound in the back of his throat.

Jackson looked down at his leather work gloves between them on the truck bench. He felt possessive of the gloves. He'd had them since his roofing days. He'd broken them in with years of sweat and grease and labor. He didn't say anything, but just slid the truck into drive and coasted forward to the next set of cans.

A few minutes later, Dean came back into the cab cradling his right hand in his left. "Sliced my finger," he said.

"Bad?" Jackson asked, trying hard to not imagine how much bacteria the cut had already absorbed.

"Not great." A drop of crimson landed on the floorboards between them.

"Christ, Dean, don't you have any work gloves?" Jackson knew he was more annoyed than he had a right to be.

Dean shook his head. He looked pathetic, glasses hanging off the edge of his nose. Another drop quickly welled up on his fingertip and hit the floor near the first.

Jackson glanced down at his gloves again. He wondered how a man like this could have handled prison. "Kent should've told you to bring gloves. The bottoms of those cans get rusted out."

"Kent didn't tell me shit." Dean stuck his finger in his mouth and sucked.

Jackson had to turn away. "Listen, take mine for today." He nudged his gloves across the bench.

Dean pushed his glasses up the slicked bridge of his nose. His face broke into a gappy smile.

"Before that," Jackson said, "let's go back to the depot and get some first aid for that finger." Though he knew—bandage or no—he would never wear those gloves again.

≈

"So what were you locked up for?" As soon as he asked the question, Jackson could tell he'd overstepped some boundary.

Dean had returned from the trailer, his finger encased in gauze and adhesive tape. He worked another cigarette from the box and shook his head, just a little. But at last he said: "Credit card fraud."

Jackson immediately became aware of his wallet, tucked into the back pocket of his jeans. This is what life had reduced him to, he thought, sharing a truck with a thief.

"How long?" he asked.

"Sentenced five years. Out in thirty-six months." Dean blew a stream of smoke at the cracked window. "You haven't ever done time, have you?"

He shook his head. "I'm a family man." They were back at Pioneer Park, and he was just turning the truck onto the access road.

"There's plenty of family men locked up in Deer Lodge." Jackson could sense that Dean had turned in his seat and was now facing him. "You want to know what it was like." It wasn't a question.

Jackson said, "You *do* realize jail is something you're supposed to be ashamed of, right?"

"Let me tell you." There was a rising note of challenge in Dean's voice. "You don't have the first idea what it was like."

Jackson felt himself getting jittery, as if he'd drunk too much caffeine—a queasy, unstable sensation that might lead to something if he wasn't careful. "I'm sure I don't *want* to know."

Mercifully, they were at the next set of cans. Jackson watched as Dean gently tugged a glove over his bandaged finger, climbed down from the truck, and began emptying the garbage.

After that, Jackson drove a little more quickly from can to can, to minimize Dean's chatter. Soon the starting and stopping became a rhythm, like a train rolling over sloppy track, or car tires chuffing over broken asphalt.

≈

Having a partner did speed the process up, and by mid-morning they'd already covered most of the city's larger parks—well ahead of schedule.

The truck CB made a sudden, noisy crackle. Kent's voice said something Jackson couldn't make out. Dean was staring at the dashboard as if it were a wild animal set loose in the cab.

"What's that, Kent? I didn't hear you," Jackson said into the mouthpiece, steering the truck with one hand.

"Just checking to make sure your new partner hadn't killed you yet." Kent's radio voice pulsed with restrained laughter.

Jackson glanced over at Dean, who looked small on the other side of the truck bench. "Not yet."

"That's some good news then." There was a short pause. "But I've got some bad news. Someone opened a packing box over by Millice Park. Goddamn Styrofoam peanuts all over the place. I want you and Dean to fix it."

The CB made a loud scratching noise and then it was silent.

≈

Even though Millice was a small park, it took the rest of the morning to clean up the mess. Jackson was grateful for the break from routine. It got him out of the truck, and it allowed him some distance from Dean. At 12:30, when they were done picking up the bits of Styrofoam, they bought fast food and took it back to the trailer at the vehicle depot.

Dean shook his head as he popped a fry into his mouth. "One thing I don't get is why you're here."

"Why does anyone do anything?" Jackson shook his head. "I've got a family. A mortgage."

"You know, me and you are the same age. I remember reading about you when I was in high school."

Jackson's stomach tightened. He hated these reminders of lost opportunity.

"All-state linebacker. Full ride scholarship to somewhere, right?" Dean chewed his food slowly and swallowed. "Not a great school, but decent good."

"So what." Jackson took a sip of his Coke and bit at the straw. There was no way scrawny Dean played a single down of meaningful football.

Dean tossed his hand in the air. "I'm just saying, a guy like you shouldn't end up stuck in Billings, Montana. Working for the parks."

"You don't know what type of guy I am."

"A guy like you should've been miles from a job like this." He sat back in his chair. "It's kinda funny. Me and you took different routes, but we ended up in the exact same place."

Jackson shrugged, but the sound of Dean's voice was like an alarm clock blaring in his ear. At the end of the summer he wouldn't even have this lousy job. How, then, would he hang on?

They were on the west end, and there was one more park to hit—Rosewood—out in a new development on the very outskirts of town, where the new construction had eaten its way toward the foothills of the Rockies. Most of the houses out here were still unoccupied, silent reminders that every boom has a bust.

As soon as Jackson pulled the truck to a stop by the first set of garbage cans, he noticed something at the far edge of the park. A gray blur that moved silently from beneath a parked car and disappeared under a trash dumpster.

"What was that?" Jackson asked.

Dean looked around the truck. "What was what?"

"Out there." He pointed, but Dean seemed uninterested.

"Let's get this park done and go home."

As Dean pulled on the gloves, Jackson saw it again. It slipped out from under the dumpster and began loping toward King Drive, which lay just beyond the park.

All at once, Jackson was out of the truck and sprinting. Dean yelled something he couldn't quite make out. He felt clean, like an engine burning lighter fluid. His legs scissored and his heart beat fiercely in his chest. He hadn't run like this in years. He wasn't panicked, necessarily; in fact, he felt strangely calm. There was something purifying in the simple motion of his body.

As Jackson came to the edge of the park he slowed down. The animal had disappeared again. Traffic on all four lanes of King Drive was steady and moving fast, and he didn't want to accidentally spook this creature into getting run over.

He whistled and said, "It's okay, boy. Where are you?"

Jackson heard nothing but the rumble of cars. He stepped cautiously toward King Drive, afraid he might discover he was too late.

Then, out of the corner of his eye, it emerged from behind a utility chest, and Jackson was in motion again. Now that he was closer, he could see it was a dog. Small, maybe a foot high, with long curly hair that had once been white.

"Here, boy," he said between gasps.

But the dog didn't seem to hear. It clearly used to be a family pet, but, lost or abandoned, it had reverted to a primitive survival state.

"It's just a goddamn dog," he heard Dean call out from somewhere behind him. "It's probably diseased. Call the pound."

Jackson tried to position himself between the dog and King Drive. He felt dizzy for a moment, lightheaded from his sprint across the park.

"Here, boy," he said again.

Jackson knew he'd have to corner and physically capture it. He wished he had his work gloves on, the ones he'd given Dean. He looked around and saw a softball backstop nearby. He stretched his arms out at his sides and began herding the dog in that direction. He was careful not to move too fast. One false start and it would head straight for the street.

"It's okay," he said. "Everything's going to be fine."

The dog was backed against the chainlink now and Jackson started to move in.

"No one's going to hurt you, boy. Everything's all right."

The dog's hair was matted. It had a filthy scent that Jackson could smell from five feet away. Underneath the fur he could see the outline of its bone structure. On its back leg it had a sore the size of a quarter.

"Good, boy." Jackson took another step. "See? I'm only trying to help."

The dog was shaking. Its dark eyes were almost hidden under a clump of dirty fur.

"It's all right now. See?" Jackson lowered himself for the grab. His knees made an arthritic pop.

The dog bolted, a whitish streak moving past his ankles. Jackson buckled to the ground. He snared the dog by its hips and held fast. The dog struggled, perhaps surprised to find it could no longer run free. Then it craned its neck. It saw Jackson's hand. It bit.

The teeth were small, but sharp. They pierced the skin and sank in deep to the bone. Jackson had to restrain an immense cry of pain. Every fiber of his body commanded him to loosen his grip, to give up. But Jackson told himself:

I will not let go. I will not let go. I will not let go.

Human Remains

My sister Collette was three years older than Marty and me. I can't really say what kind of person or sister she was. I only recall fragments of memory. If you were to fit them all together, they might make up a whole picture, a true picture. But to me the pieces are what matter.

She had a Fischer-Price record player that spun plastic records. At night, before her bedtime, she'd sneak into our room.

"This next song goes out to a young man who had a tough day," she'd intone into her giraffe hairbrush. "My brother Jack scraped his knee on the playground, so let's play him a song that'll make his spirit shine." She'd usually play "Camptown Races" for me, even though I didn't much care for the tune.

"What about me?" Marty would ask as soon as it was over. "Okay, very nice," Collette would say into the giraffe brush. "I'm going to end my set tonight with a dedication to the bravest young guy out there. Marty, there's no reason to be afraid of the dark. Remember that." Then she'd play "Twinkle Twinkle, Little Star."

Most nights I'd fall asleep before it finished. Every once in a while, though, I'd stay awake until the end. The last few notes would flatten as the spring mechanism finished unspooling. She'd quietly gather her records and the record player and the giraffe brush, and slip out of the room, down the hall, like a ghost taking leave of the haunted.

This was a memory I returned to often during that summer we built the canoe on the Upper Peninsula.

≈

"Today's an important day on your journey," Big Angus said the morning of the fourth weekend. "We're gonna install the manboards in your canoes."

By then, we were down to three groups of builders. The frat brothers from the University of Michigan had gone to a bar called The Malamute one night and started a fight with some locals. None of them came back after that. Big Angus had left their partially finished canoe in place next to the Caspers', the Wetzels', and ours.

Now he held up a piece of wood that had been built by layering dozens of flat pieces together and bending them into an S-shape. The manboard looked like it took days to construct, so everyone was relieved to see that Big Angus and Eugene had already built them for us.

"We call it a manboard because it looks kinda like a man squatting," he said. "See, there's his shoulders."

We all chuckled, even if we didn't quite see the resemblance.

"The manboard is what gives the canoe its strength," Big Angus said. "If it's not in there good, the whole thing's gonna fall apart." Eugene showed us how to attach it. The process meant stitching the manboard to the bark of the canoe using moistened jackpine root.

In order to thread the jackpine root through the eyelets, you had to get in really close to make sure you were doing it right. It was incredibly tedious work. Bruised knuckles, sliced skin, swollen joints. Marty and I tried to pitch in, but there was only so much we could do. I could tell my parents were in pain because they got really quiet. I knew what it meant when they were loud. Loud I could deal with. It was the quiet that scared me most.

≈

That night I couldn't fall asleep. My body was radiating pain. I could feel my hands throbbing. Mom was having a hard time sleeping too. She kept turning and rolling, the nylon of her sleeping bag rubbing against the tent floor. Later, very late, I heard the tent zipper slide open and my mother crawl out. I gave her a half-minute head start, then followed.

She wasn't going fast, so I easily caught up. It was a bright moon. I could make out her silhouette as she walked through the forest. Eventually, she came to the edge of Lake Michigan. Without hesitating, she strode into the water until the surface lapped at the bottoms of her kneecaps. She stood there, holding her elbows to her ribs for warmth, looking out at the lake like she expected an answer to a question.

A breeze kicked up. The moon cast her impossibly slim shadow across the riffled water. I started to worry, convinced that something was about to happen that might alter everything again.

"Mom," I whispered from the shore.

She spun and stared at me. Her eyes were black.

"Don't be afraid," I said. "It's me."

I could see her relax. She began walking back toward me.

"You're supposed to be asleep," she said.

"Is the water cold?" I asked.

"It feels good," she said. "I'm sore from today." She stood on the shore and knelt down. She plunged her hands into the water and said, "You should try it."

I knelt beside her and did the same. The cold bit at first, but then it felt as if it was leaching the pain away.

"Sometimes it feels like our family's haunted," I said.

"Not haunted," she said. "Cursed maybe."

It was quiet for a moment. I heard the yip of a coyote carrying across the water.

"I didn't mean to scare you," my mother said. "Being in the water like that."

"What do you do when you can't sleep?" I asked.

"I remember," she said. "Mostly, I remember."

≈

What happened to Collette was so simple it defies comprehension. Dad's friend from work, Mr. Frankel, was going out of town for a week and said we could stay at his place. His house was nice, and we weren't the type of family that could afford to go on a real vacation.

In Mr. Frankel's backyard, he had a pool shaped like a lima bean. Every morning we'd pack up towels and sunscreen and a picnic lunch and walk out the back door as if we were spending a day at the beach.

"Like a fancy resort," my dad would remind us, and we all nodded, even though our own house was only fifteen minutes away.

The exact moment it happened, I can't say what we were doing. Were my parents arguing? Were Marty and I complaining? Was there some other distraction? All I know is that four of us were outside the pool and one of us was in it. My dad was the first to recognize the silence, how long it was. He jumped up when he saw Collette floating motionless, her hair waving across the surface of the water like seaweed. Dad dove in. He dragged her out. He started to resuscitate her.

"Jack, call 9-1-1! Call 9-1-1!"

I went inside. I dialed. The operator asked for Mr. Frankel's address, and I didn't know it. I had no idea. I looked around and looked around, and then I ran out front with the cordless phone and looked at the street number, and still I didn't know the street, and I didn't know what else to do so I barged back inside and almost tripped over Marty, and finally I saw a pile of mail, and I had to read it off from that. It felt like it took forever.

Out by the pool, my mother was still sitting in her deck chair. She was shivering. Dad was still doing CPR, but Collette looked less and less like a person who had ever been alive.

"She's playing," Marty said. "It's a joke. She's playing. It's not real. Collette, stop joking. Open your eyes. It's not funny anymore. Open your eyes."

My mother raised her head to look at Marty. Her gaze was narrow. When she spoke, I couldn't recognize her voice. "What did you do to prevent this?" she asked. "Tell me one goddamn thing."

Marty shut his mouth. Dad stopped trying to bring Collette back. Her wet hair was tangled around her shoulders.

Some time later, I realized mom wasn't talking to just Marty. We were all complicit in what happened that day—all four of us guilty as a band of thieves.

≈

The next morning I woke to an empty tent. When I climbed outside, my mom was hunched over the camp stove, turning scrambled eggs in an iron skillet.

"Where's Dad and Marty?" I asked.

"At the lake," she said over her shoulder. "Bathing."

"She used to play records for us," I said. "At night. Before bed, on that record player she had."

My mom didn't say anything for what seemed like a very long time.

"That's what I remember," I said.

"You should eat, Jack." She grabbed a plate and put some eggs on it. "You must be starving."

A few minutes later, Dad and Marty came back to the camp, rowdy and hale from their plunge into the cold water.

"That felt great," Dad said.

"Darn tootin'," Marty chimed in. It was a phrase he'd started using recently. No one knew where he'd picked it up from.

"You two should try it," Dad said. "I can't recommend it enough."

"I made breakfast," my mom said. She prepared plates and then climbed back into the tent. She didn't come out until it was time to work on the canoe.

≈

"Today's an important day in the life of your canoe," Big Angus told us that morning when the groups had assembled.

"He says that every day," Marty whispered to me.

"Maybe every day *is* important," I said.

"Today we're gonna really find out how good you've been putting your canoe together." He looked from the Wetzels, to the Caspers, to us. I always got the impression Big Angus saw more than was immediately visible.

"It's time to take out the temporary frame. That's how we're gonna really see what's what. If you've built it right, your canoe should hold its shape. If not, well, there's probably nothing we can do to save it."

An anxious murmur broke out among the remaining groups. We'd invested serious time in this project, not to mention cost. To have that all evaporate right before our eyes seemed cruel. It felt like a larger judgment.

Removal of the temporary frame was tricky. We had to dismantle it while it was still inside the boat, then slide the long pieces out through a gap in the stitching at the front. It required the assistance of both Big Angus and Eugene, so we had to do it one canoe at a time.

The first group to go was the Wetzels. They pulled the nails from the frame and then stood back as Big Angus and Eugene stepped in to work the timbers loose. You could see the caution in their movements. They did nothing without testing the reaction first. Occasionally, Eugene would knock on a piece and, depending on the sound it made, they'd either loosen it, or move to another piece.

Then it came time to slide out the long boards. They did it in one smooth motion. When they were done, the canoe held its shape. It looked light and buoyant on the ground. Big Angus shook hands with the Wetzels—father, mother, three girls. He whispered something into each of their ears, and they smiled. Then he moved on to the Caspers.

From the beginning, it was clear their canoe was in trouble. Big Angus and Eugene were more cautious. They spent more time knocking on the timbers, searching for the right one to pull out first. They kept shaking their heads. The look on the Caspers' faces got darker. Even the two boys, younger than Marty and me, could sense the verdict would be grim.

At last, Big Angus and Eugene took the long timber on the port side and worked it loose. Immediately, the shell of the canoe started to warp. The men tried to put the support back in place, but it was too late. The entire sheet of bark tore loose from its stitching and leapt into the air as if a huge snare had been sprung.

"I'm sorry," Big Angus said. "Sometimes things are beyond saving."

The Caspers were staring at the broken wreckage of their canoe. All their work was now just kindling.

"If you'd like to try again next summer, maybe we could work something out," Big Angus offered.

The Caspers nodded, but I could tell they were defeated. They'd never come back here again.

"Okay," Big Angus said. "One more to go."

My dad was pacing alongside our canoe, wringing his hands and muttering. Marty and I looked anxiously at each other. I knew I didn't want to be the one to go first. As long as we did nothing, we'd never have to know. Then all at once, my mother picked up a hammer and began clawing at the nails in the frame.

"Be careful, Jeannie," Dad said. "Jesus."

"Let's just get this over with," she said without looking up.

When the nails were out, Big Angus and Eugene stepped in. I couldn't read their body language. They'd knock on a timber and move on. Knock again, test it, move on. I think they genuinely didn't know how ours would turn out.

Finally, a decision was soundlessly made. They grasped the starboard timber, shifted it back and forth, then unwedged it. The birch bark hull made a ticking noise as it started to pull against the stitching.

Before it had a chance to settle, Big Angus and Eugene unwedged the second long timber, slipped it out, and stood back.

The canoe sat there. We all watched it like something that was newly hatched, barely clinging to life. My father instinctively grabbed all of us—me, Marty, my mom. He encircled us with his arms and pulled us close, not a hug so much as a gathering in.

The canoe made violin string sounds. The bark skin trembled. The gunwales twitched. And then it stopped. Before I even realized we were in the clear, Big Angus was shaking our hands.

When he shook mine, he bent down and whispered into my ear: "It continues."

A little while later, I asked Marty what Big Angus had said to him. Marty looked at me kind of funny, as if I'd asked him something deeply personal, which, in retrospect, I had.

Marty cupped his hand and whispered in my ear. "He said, 'You are the bravest one of all.'"

≈

My father was giddy that night as we ate our dinner—spaghetti and meatballs from a can.

"Did you see that thing?" he asked. "We slid those boards out and—ping, ting—it held tight, like the head of a drum." He was waving his hands in outsized gestures. "That's craftsmanship. That's workmanship. That's…that's art."

While Dad was highly animated, our mother was the opposite. She stared quietly at the campfire. She held her plate of spaghetti, but hadn't touched it.

Like most children, I was largely governed by my parents' moods. So this type of situation posed a quandary. Part of me felt drawn to Dad's exuberance. But another part knew it was unfair to celebrate when Mom clearly wasn't inclined to it. Marty and I sat quietly on a log next to each other, eating our spaghetti.

"Don't get me wrong, I feel bad for the Caspers," Dad went on. "But I could tell the whole time their canoe was wrong. It looked off. But ours, man, I knew it. True lines, clean stitching. You can't make it better than that. Big Angus knew. So did Eugene. They knew we'd made a good one. It was obvious."

"Would you please be quiet?" my mom said.

The fire popped between us. Embers floated into the sky.

"I'm happy, Jeannie. I'm proud of our accomplishment."

"Please, please stop talking."

I could see the metal camp plate shaking in her hands.

"In three days it will be two years." My mom's voice sounded brittle.

Dad took a moment to respond. "I know, Jeannie. I'm aware of that."

"Are you?"

Dad glanced at Marty and me. "I am."

Without warning, my mother whipped her plate into the forest. The spaghetti fell off and landed in a tangle in the dirt, and the plate flew like a Frisbee and disappeared into the darkness. A split-second later, we heard a clang as it hit a tree. "Then why didn't you say anything?" she asked.

"I don't know," my dad said. "I thought... I don't know."

"Two years ago," my mother said. She was looking at her hands, which she held out in front of her. There was sauce on one, but she didn't wipe it off. "Two years almost to the day. They say you're supposed to feel better. I don't feel better. I feel worse. So much worse."

She dropped her hands onto her lap. I looked at the campfire for a moment. In the distance, I could hear the Wetzel girls singing a song, but I didn't recognize the tune.

"What did Big Angus whisper to you guys?" It was Marty, using his Human Hologram voice.

I wasn't sure if anyone was going to answer him, but then my mother said, "You want to know what he said to me?" She gave out a hard-edged laugh. "He said, 'You are all forgiven.'" My mother paused as if the line needed a minute to sink in.

"I think that's nice," Dad said. "That's something we all need to hear."

"What a crock of shit," my mother said, and then she suddenly stood up. She seemed unnaturally tall between us. The glow from the campfire cast upward shadows on her face. She didn't look like my mother in that moment.

"Here's what Big Angus should have told us: 'None of you small people deserve to be alive.'"

"That's enough," my dad said.

"Yes it is," my mom said. "Yes, it is quite enough."

≈

She spent the night in the car. My dad, Marty, and I slept in the tent. None of us made mention of the fact that she was separate from us.

"What did Mom mean?" Marty asked, just as a quiet was settling on the tent.

"I don't really know," my dad said.

"You don't?" Marty sounded scared at this prospect.

"Sometimes people say things they don't really mean."

"Do we deserve to be alive?"

My dad didn't say anything. I could hear him breathing, and I thought for a moment he might have fallen asleep.

"Dad?" Marty asked again.

"Yes," he said. "Everyone does." Then he rolled over, and I knew he'd said all he could on the matter.

I lay in the sleeping bag, ears attuned to every noise the night offered. I could hear the scurrying of nocturnal animals, the groan of the trees, the distant lapping of the lake at the shore. I startled at the occasional pop from the embers of our campfire. But I did not hear what I really wanted to hear—the sound of my mother returning to us, or the sound of my father getting up to go to her.

≈

My mother didn't join us after we assembled at the canoes the next morning, either. When I asked dad about her, he said, "She needs space right now, Jack. We need to give her space."

Big Angus came out of his trailer and inspected the two remaining groups. He didn't seem surprised to see my mother wasn't with us. I'm not sure if he'd heard what had happened last night, or if he'd always sensed our fragility and known that, sooner or later, a rupture like this would happen.

"We're close now," Big Angus told the groups. "Today we're gonna fit the cedar ribs in place to strengthen your vessel. Once that's done she'll be able to withstand any storm you might find on these waters." He adjusted his hunting cap and pushed his glasses up the bridge of his nose. "One more weekend after this, and you're done."

Compared to installing the manboard, fitting the ribs in place was easy. A simple matter of trimming them and sliding them in until they were tight. Still, Big Angus paid more attention to us than usual. Normally, this would have chafed my father, to be singled out for assistance, but I could tell he was grateful for the extra help.

When we were done that afternoon, we went back and found that my mother had packed up our camp. The tent, sleeping bags, and cookware were all stowed in the Gran Torino.

The campfire was scattered, the laundry packed. She'd been so thorough that you could hardly tell a family had spent the last three days living in that clearing.

My mother was waiting in the passenger seat.

No one spoke while my dad got behind the wheel, and Marty and I climbed into the way back. As we crossed the Mackinac Bridge, heading back to the mainland, Marty and I stared out the curved glass of the back window, unsure of what we were leaving behind.

Eureka, California

My name is Lewis Montgomery Lapin, but most people call me Trigger. I always put up a fight about it, tell people how much I hate that nickname. But they point out that I'm a high-strung type of guy and Trigger just fits better than Lewis. And eventually I give up trying to correct them. You can't change something that cuts so close to who you are.

I'd only been living in Eureka a month before people at my new job picked up on the nickname. I was surveying for an engineering company that designs roads and sewer systems in the forests of northern California. Before this, I'd been doing construction in LA, but things went bad for me down there and I had to leave. It had been the usual shit: some outstanding debts, problems with my girlfriend Sherise, and even a few legal issues that're really best not to get into. Basically the kind of stuff that'll dog a guy no matter where he finds himself. Eureka has a population of about 25,000 people, so I figured it might be a good place for me to get straight after LA. I was all about the fresh start.

My job with Imhoff Engineering was pretty sweet. Most of it involved wandering around the forests, surveying sites for construction projects. They've got computers and GPS stuff to do all the heavy brainwork now, so things were nice and simple. The worst part of the job was that I was partnered up with this tight-ass named Slate. He was one of those conservative types who calls himself a libertarian. Whatever *that* means. He was always listening to these wind-baggy radio shows and bitching about how the government's ruining the country. We were an odd couple. But in a way, I think Slate was a good influence on me. His tight-assedness helped me curb some of my wilder ways, which was what I'd been planning on doing by going to Eureka in the first place. So, overall, I had few complaints about my setup.

The first week in August, Slate and I were slogging along this forest trail, trying to get some topo readings for a new logging road. It was a hot Friday afternoon and we were pretty much off the maps. Redwoods rose up like giant towers, so big around the two of us together couldn't have stretched our arms around them. When you get deep into the forest like that, things take on a different feel. The air crackles with the sounds of birds chirping and unseen animals slipping through the undergrowth. It's peaceful in a way. But occasionally it can drive me a little psycho. If I'm not careful with silences like that, I get trapped inside my head, which is not always a pleasant place to be. Sometimes I just wish I could hear the sound of an ambulance siren or the reassuring rumble of a trash compactor to break up all that weird nature-silence and the thoughts and memories flashing through my brain.

We were walking along this trail and it was stinking hot out. I was in the lead, carrying a tripod with a scope on top. It was heavy and awkward, and it kept getting snagged on the brush. Slate was whistling some church tune with that kind of hollow sound people make when they're not a good whistler. I was fighting my way through a patch of tall ferns, trying to wrestle the branches out of my face, when the ground went spongy underneath me. It must've rained earlier that day because I was on a slope of slick, wet vegetation and every move I made caused me to slip further down the hill.

I turned to Slate and tried to reach out for his hand, but I missed, and gravity had its way with me. I started picking up speed down the hill, like a skier who's in over his head. Eventually, I tossed the tripod to the side and tucked into a roll, and everything went green until I landed on my back on a soft patch of dirt.

"You all right down there, Trigger?" Even Slate, the conservative tight-ass, called me Trigger, which, I have to say, surprised me a little. He never struck me as the nickname type. Slate was his real, God-given name.

"Yeah," I called up to him. I stood up and dusted myself off. "I think everything's going to be all right."

When Slate got down to where I was, he took a look around. "Well, I'll be darned," he said. He was shaking his head slowly. "Son of a gun."

All around us was a field of pot plants. At least a couple hundred big ones, planted in neat little rows.

I should probably mention here that Eureka is in Humboldt County, which they say is the best place in all of America for growing marijuana. In the local bars, you'd hear stories about fields like this one—how they're run by Mexican cartels and patrolled by wetbacks carrying sawed-offs. Last year a couple college boys from San Francisco came up and wandered into one of these fields and started acting like kids on Halloween. Their bodies were found a few days later in a reservoir outside town. Their tongues had been cut out and shoved down their throats.

"Looks pretty crazy here, eh, Slate?" I said, mostly because I didn't know what else to say. Even though I'd heard that story about the college boys, I started to get a little bit of an idea. I mean, here I was, standing in a field of dope. It's hard not to start mentally drooling when you find yourself in a situation like that. Even if common sense is screaming at you otherwise.

Slate walked over to one of the plants and kicked at it. He rubbed his hand over his sweaty flat top. "We'll have to report this," he said.

"It sure is a shame," I said, trying to sound all disapproving.

"How's that?"

"Well, you know, we'll call it in, and the government'll just come out here and confiscate everything." I'd listened to enough of Slate's radio shows to know that this little ploy might have some traction with him. "Some crooked DEA agent will probably turn around and re-sell it. Make themselves a nice tidy profit."

Slate had his cell phone out and he'd already punched in a few numbers and I have to admit my heart was starting to sag. But sometimes, when you think for sure a guy will do one thing, he'll turn right around and do the opposite.

He put the phone down and looked at me for a minute. I think he saw some kind of hunger in my eyes that tipped him off.

"You know, Trigger, if you were to take something from here and if I didn't notice, there's probably nothing anybody could do about it." He had a smile on his craggy face. And right then, if I could have, I would've nominated him for sainthood.

I went over to the nearest plant and grabbed it by its stringy stalk and pulled it out of the ground, roots and all. I did that to two more plants. The root balls were heavy with black soil and the plants were big, so three was all I could manage. I tucked one of them under my arm and carried the other two in my hands.

I crawled up the hill and started hoofing it back down the trail to where we'd parked the company truck. As I was running, all those crazy forest sounds were pounding in my ears. I started to imagine those wetbacks were out there watching, training their rifles on me, picking out a bead, leading my movements, adjusting for the wind.

When people call me Trigger and point out that I'm high-strung, there's not much I can say to argue with them. See, I get this thing going inside me which I call the Skeebers. First, my guts start flopping around like a net full of fish tossed onto a riverbank. Then the Skeebers work their way up through my chest 'til my lungs feel like inflated balloons. And then finally they get to my heart, which begins hammering away so hard I can feel it in my temples. I usually get the Skeebers when I'm doing something I know I shouldn't. It's like I'm watching myself doing dumb shit, and there's nothing I can do to stop it.

It was a mile and a half sprint to the truck. During the twenty minutes it took me to get there, it's safe to say I experienced an onset of the Skeebers. I reached the truck and looked around to make sure no one had followed me. My legs and arms felt like rubber bands and I had a sour taste in my mouth. But I was in the clear. So I pulled a bunch of heavy-duty trash bags from the pickup and triple-wrapped the pot plants. Then I hid them in the bed of the pickup underneath a bunch of old tools and lumber.

I was halfway back to the pot field when I ran into Slate. He was walking casually, all cool smiles and church tune-whistling.

"I called it in," he said. "It's not our problem anymore." Then he looked at his watch. "It's late. We ought to get back to the office."

≈

When we pulled into the company parking lot I told Slate to go on ahead. I then transferred the garbage bags into the bed of my own pickup.

Inside, Slate was standing near the water cooler, sipping from a big plastic mug. He was telling some of our coworkers about the pot field and how he'd reported it. He said it all with a look of real serious disgust, as if he couldn't decide which he hated more, the pot growers, or the fact that he'd had to call it in to the government.

Eventually our coworkers cleared out and it was just Slate and me standing at the cooler. "You might want to get those scratches checked out," he said.

I looked at my arms and saw just how badly I'd gotten nicked when I took my fall. The scratches were deep. Blood had leaked from them and clotted in brown streaks on my skin. My face felt pretty raw too. (Only when I looked at it later in a mirror would I see how badly it had been messed up. Suffice to say, I wasn't the prettiest guy in the world anymore. Not that I was ever Mr. Good-Looking to begin with.)

"Any big plans for the weekend, Trigger?" Slate asked over the rim of his mug.

"Can't say as I do. Probably just chill."

"That's good," he said. "You be careful now."

It was funny, but somehow over the whole pot field incident, we'd bonded. I think Slate looked at me the way you'd look at a son who you love, but who just does the wrong thing every now and again.

≈

When I got home that night, I hauled the pot plants into the basement. They were green and moist, and I knew I had to dry them out before I could do anything. So I strung them from a ceiling beam with wire coat hangers and then just looked at them. They were beautiful, in a way. They hung down like three velvety cave bats, their tips almost touching the floor.

There'd be enough dope on those babies to last me a good long while. I'd have a monster stash that wouldn't run out for years. Because that was my plan. Completely selfish. I was going to keep that pot for myself, maybe share it with a few select friends when they came by. I didn't officially have any friends in Eureka yet, but I knew that was going to change soon. We'd crank some tunes, smoke up, and bliss out. The American Dream. At least my own personal version of it.

Of course I'd have to wait a while for the plants to dry out. Which was an arrangement I was cool with. But I couldn't deny that I still felt that case of the Skeebers jumping and flopping in my stomach.

I spent the weekend locked inside my house. But I wanted to tell someone about my good fortune. I mean, how can you keep something like this to yourself? I considered calling Sherise down in LA. I even dialed her number once or twice, but then hung up when she picked up the phone. In the end, I decided she probably wouldn't share my enthusiasm for my little windfall. Especially since, when I left LA, it wasn't exactly on the best of terms with regard to our relationship. No, probably best to not tell her about the pot.

So I just strutted and fretted all weekend long. All by myself.

≈

That next week at work I tried to lay low. Slate and I went out into the field twice. Things were fine between us. I acted completely normal, and he listened to his radio shows and griped about this or that. It was only the days when I was at the office that I felt a little heat. Not directly. More like conversations I'd overhear in the lunchroom or in the hallway outside my cubicle. I determined to mind my own business and play dumb.

One thing I've noticed: *being* dumb is easy; it's a lot harder to *play* dumb.

But I kept my cool and I waited. And each day my cave bats got drier and drier. I could see their leaves turning gray. Crystals formed on the buds like frost on the morning grass. I started calling them my Little Bundles of Joy. I named them Patsy, Jude and Clementine. I started feeling bad for the day I'd have to trim them down and wrap them up and put them away in my freezer. But I didn't get silly about it. I've learned it's best in life to avoid emotional attachments; they can really snare a guy if he isn't careful.

Also, my scratches weren't healing great. In fact, they weren't healing at all. If I'd've been smart, I would've put some peroxide or Mercurochrome on them right away. But in all the excitement, I'd totally forgotten about it. Pus started to form in the scratches, kind of yellowy and hot. I wore bandages to keep them hidden, even though it made me look like a mummy. And then they'd start itching like nothing you'd ever believe. It was a crazy burning itch I could not shake. I'd squirm in my seat at work, willing myself to let well enough alone. Then at night, I'd get home from work, rip off the bandages and start scratching away like I was sharpening my nails on my own skin.

Of course, my scratching only caused them to run with blood all over again. So I'd let them breathe a while before I had to wrap them up for work the next day. It was a cycle I could not break.

≈

I think the whole thing would have worked out great except for one thing: my truck. That goddamn piece-of-shit Chevy. Why did I ever get that thing? I should have gotten a Ford. Any fool would have told me that. Maybe the fact that I had a Chevy is proof positive that I am an incurable imbecile.

I was driving home from work in my Chevy a few weeks after my tumble into the pot field. All at once, I heard this thumpa-thumpa coming from underneath somewhere. Then the thumpa-thumpa turned into this loud clanking for a few seconds and finally it turned into a grinding shriek. Metal on metal.

I pulled over and called a tow truck from the payphone at the gas station on the corner. The mechanic looked at my rig and determined that it was my transmission. Excuse me? Transmission? How much is that going to cost?

"Twenty-five hundred bucks," he said in this calm, flat tone like a doctor who's telling you the final curtain is nigh. From where I stood, "twenty-five hundred bucks" sounded like "emphysema" or "pancreatic cancer."

I left the mechanic's shop and walked home—at least two miles—all the way hanging my head in defeat, practically crying. The thing is, it's like three miles from my house to work each morning. And there's no such thing as public transportation in a town like Eureka. So I was in a pretty bad spot, being pickup-less and all.

I kicked around my house that evening and checked on my Little Bundles of Joy. They were drying quite nicely by now. In fact, they were basically ready for trimming. And as I inspected them—walking around them, poking at them, sniffing the buds—a plan began to form in my head. Slowly at first, like, I can't do that. But then, wait, maybe. And on and on until yes, perfect, that should work without a hitch.

≈

The next day I jogged into work at five in the morning, before anybody would be there. I scribbled a note and left it on Slate's desk. It said something like: "Gordon wants me to recheck the data points on Lot 46 up near the Beaver Creek Project." I signed it, "All the best, Trigger." And I put a smiley face next to my name with a little wink, which was meant to say, Hey, even though this may not be entirely kosher, please just cover for me.

On my way out the door, I slipped a set of keys for one of the company trucks off the pegboard they keep near the lunchroom.

It wasn't a normal by-the-books plan, to be sure. But I was making the best of a rotten situation. That's what I always do. (As for why I'd ended up in the rotten situation in the first place, that's a philosophical question I'd rather not get into. But clearly gravity had something to do with it.)

≈

Soon I was driving south on the 101, right down the spine of California in a white pickup truck with "Imhoff Engineering" printed on the sides. In the seat next to me were three plain-wrapped packages filled with the dope I'd cut from Patsy, Jude and Clementine. I'd had to hack my Little Bundles of Joy into tiny pieces until all that was left were the valuable parts. To be precise, there were about three pounds' worth of valuable parts. And those little gems would be my ticket to a new transmission.

It felt good to be out there driving. Though I'll admit that the low-level Skeebers I'd been feeling ever since my interlude in the pot field had kicked into overdrive. My stomach was doing a gymnastics routine—bounce, flip, bounce—with every mile I crept southward. And my heart was pumping like one of those rubber balls that Slate kept at his desk to relieve stress.

I drank coffee until about nine, then switched over to Mountain Dew. By noon, the cab of the pickup was strewn with cans. I figured that piss stops were really eating into my progress, so I bought a gallon jug of fresh spring water, which I promptly dumped out and then used as my own personal port-o-potty. It was a hell of a setup, no doubt, and the smell was not pretty, but these were desperate straits and I was in them up to my neck.

At a gas station outside Oakland I called an old buddy of mine from my LA days. Tiny was a good guy at heart. He was involved in some of the less savory aspects of life—that's the nicest way I can put it. And he'd been a big part of the reason I'd had to leave. But he was a guy who would know how to move what I was bringing with me.

The phone rang and rang. And just when I had given up hope, Tiny picked up. He seemed pissed that I'd woken him, but when I explained the opportunity I'd stumbled into, he said he might be able to help.

Driving down to LA and talking to Tiny put me in the mood of my former days. And once those memories were stirred up, my thoughts turned to another certain someone who I shared those LA days with: Sherise. It seemed like it would be a tragedy to go all the way down there and not look her up.

I hadn't been with another woman since Sherise, and I have to admit, I was feeling some manly urges. I knew she might not be super-pleased to see me, but it seemed like things were turning my way, and I figured she'd want to be a part of that, once she knew all the facts. So at the next gas stop, near Fresno, I dialed her number.

It rang three times before a creaky answering machine clicked on. After the beep, I said, "Hey, there, Sherise. This is your old buddy, Lewis." Sherise, unlike most people, never called me Trigger, a fact which I've always held to her credit. "I'm going to be stopping by LA for a little business. If you're free, I might have an hour or two when we could get together. Maybe coffee or something else. If you're free."

Coffee! Ha! I couldn't believe the way that sounded after I'd said it. So sophisticated. Yes, this was what adults did. They got together over coffee and rehashed a few sweet memories before parting ways and sailing off into the night.

≈

I rolled into LA around three in the afternoon. I was to meet up with Tiny at this little bar in West Hollywood called The Sweet Hereafter. As I walked inside, into the cool dark air, I got all soft for the olden days. There was the same velvet picture of the naked mermaid over the bar. The same high-backed barstools made out of red Naugahyde. It was a genuine homecoming.

I even recognized the woman tending bar. Her name was Marion. She had this wild dyed-blonde hair that was perpetually frozen in a bad perm. She was an older lady and she was a tough one, no doubt. She had overseen some of our more festive evenings at The Sweet Hereafter. She had put up with a lot of our grief over the years, but she always took it in a good-natured way. I really loved that woman.

"What're you drinking?" she asked when I took a seat at the bar.

She didn't recognize me. That made sense, though. It had been a while. And my hair used to be a lot longer too. I'd cut it after moving to Eureka—not too short like Slate's, but decent-looking, respectable.

"Remember me?" I asked, all chipper and eager. "Lewis Lapin."

Then I saw it dawning on her. "Trigger," she said. "You back in town?"

"Only for a little while. Just taking care of some business."

She nodded at this, one hand resting on the bar. Then she turned and started filling a mug with icy cold beer. When she set it in front of me, she squinted, peering close as if she were trying to solve a long division problem on my forehead.

"What happened to your face, Trigger?" she asked.

I touched my cheek and felt the hot lines of the scratches. "Had an accident," I said. "You know me, clumsy as ever."

She shrugged her shoulders and scrunched up her nose. "You might want to get those things checked out. They look infected."

I laughed at this, though it was only after I laughed that I realized she hadn't meant it to be funny.

"I'll be all right. You know me, I always pull through."

She agreed with this and then drifted down to the other end of the bar where two fat guys were watching CNN with the sound turned down. Poor Marion. She looked a lot older than I'd remembered. Sagging lines on her face. And her hair was worn out from all the bleaching she'd put it through.

I was starting to work on my third or fourth beer when Tiny showed up and took a seat at the stool next to mine. Lots of guys get called "Tiny" because they're actually big dudes. My Tiny, however, is exactly what his name would suggest. He's short and scrawny, with a sharp-looking ferret face.

"Been a while, Trigger," he said. His shoulders were slumped, which made him look even smaller.

"Too long," I said.

He seemed wary of me. He hadn't even shaken my hand. Maybe Tiny was mad about the way I'd left town in such a rush all those months ago. People can get bitter over the smallest things; it's like an illness. I make it a point to never hold grudges, and I think that philosophy has served me well over the years.

"So you brought something with you?" he asked. Marion had put a glass of beer in front of him, but he hadn't touched it yet. He was working his hands together as if his palms were sweaty.

"I sure did, Tiny. But I just got here. No point getting down to business right away."

"What did you have in mind?" he asked.

"I don't know! Hang out for a bit. Tip a few beers. Talk about the olden days."

He looked at me with those narrow eyes of his. "Olden days? What, like six months ago?"

"Sure," I said. I was starting to run out of patience with his attitude. If he wanted to hold a grudge, fine. But let's at least be civil. "How've you been, Tiny?"

"Shitty," he said. He was still worming his hands together and it was making me nervous. "What the hell is wrong with your face, man?"

I touched my scratches, which had begun to itch again. "Nothing. I had an accident a few weeks ago. It'll clear up in no time."

"You look like hell, Trigger."

This had officially turned into one crappy homecoming. I don't mind telling you I felt lower than low right then. Tiny, my buddy, my comrade-in-arms, was showing a distinct lack of hospitality.

"Don't you remember all the great times?" I asked. "Aren't those worth anything anymore?"

"They're worth about a squirt of piss, old buddy." He laughed at this, all mean-like, his ferret face scrunched up and nasty.

"Listen," I said. "If you don't want to chat, that's cool with me. We can just take care of business and call it a day."

"Works for me," he said. He picked up his beer and chugged it. Three monstrous swallows that made you wonder how such a scrawny dude can put that much beer in him so fast. Then: "Where's the stuff?"

"Out in my pickup."

He shook his head. "Always the brilliant one, Trigger. Three pounds of dope and you leave it in a car in the parking lot. Real smart."

We stood up and walked out of The Sweet Hereafter and into the blazing LA sun. He laughed again when he saw "Imhoff Engineering" on the side of my pickup. "Real smart," he said.

I was getting sick of Tiny's laugh at this point, and I had half a mind to knock a couple of his teeth out. But I also had an eye on my mission. After all, I had a plan, and, sour homecoming or not, I had to stick with it.

"This truck smells like piss," he said when I opened the door. He looked at the jug I'd been using for my port-o-potty. "I'm not even going to ask."

"I'm certainly thankful for that, Tiny."

I fished the packages out of the truck and carried them over to Tiny's car—some 80s-vintage heap. We stowed them in the trunk and he pulled out a fat envelope, which he handed to me.

"Three grand," he said through his teeth. "You can count it if you like."

"Not necessary among old friends," I said. I was keeping up the old-friends bit mostly just to annoy him.

He slammed his trunk and shook my hand, a gesture I was grateful for, I have to admit. And, with that, he climbed into his car and drove off. I watched him go, thinking, So long, Patsy, Jude and Clementine. I hope things work out well for you kids.

It was three in the afternoon, and my plan had gone off smoothly enough. The Skeebers I'd been feeling all morning quieted down noticeably. But I couldn't deny that I was feeling a little hollow over the shabby way Tiny had treated me. I don't know. I guess I wanted something more from this expedition. Going home now, even with the necessary cash, would still feel like I was going home empty-handed. I resolved to call Sherise one more time to see if she was around.

Again there was no answer. So I figured, What the heck, I'll just stop on by real quick and see if she's around. Her place wasn't far from The Sweet Hereafter so it would be no trouble at all.

≈

Sherise's apartment complex was one of those depressing two-story buildings with a pool that no one ever cleaned. But we'd had some good times there nonetheless. We'd lit that place up, Sherise and me. That's the way we were—always making the best of some pretty rotten situations. God, when things were going well between us, they were really unbelievable, I can assure you.

The front gate, as usual, was unlocked. So I pushed my way in and walked right up to Sherise's door.

Ding-dong.

Silence.

Knock, knock.

Finally some shuffling noises coming from somewhere inside. Then the knob twisted and the door crept open. At first all I could see was this kind of heavy gloom inside. Then, as my eyes adjusted to the dark, I saw her.

Sherise was not looking so great. She was bone skinny, and pale as a corpse. She had these dark circles under her eyes that I'd never seen in all the days when we were together.

"Surprise!" I said, trying to sound genuinely happy. "Bet you never expected to see me again."

She drew her breath in. Not sharply, but kind of slowly as if she wasn't sure how her lungs were supposed to work.

"Lewis," she said, "what happened to your face?"

"Oh, don't worry about that. I work for an engineering company these days. Surveying, Sherise. Lots of tromping around in the forests up north. You get nicked up occasionally. Nothing a little time can't heal." I touched my face and felt the scratches. They were hot and a few of them were running again. Had I scratched at them on the car ride over? I couldn't remember.

"What are you doing here?" She had her arms wrapped around her chest. Her fingers were digging into her biceps.

"I left a message earlier. I guess you didn't get it. I was just passing through town on some business and I thought I'd pop on over to say hi. Maybe we could go grab a coffee or something. I'm due back in Eureka pretty soon, but I should be able to hang out for an hour or so. What do you say? Coffee. My treat."

"I got your message, Lewis. I don't think it would be a great idea right now."

"Sherise, let's not let the past fuzz up the present. I'd really like to talk for a bit. See how you're doing."

"How I'm doing?" She stepped back from the door, but I don't think she was inviting me in. Besides, I didn't really want to go inside her apartment anymore. It looked so gloomy in there, so dark and depressing. I stepped backwards so she'd feel more free to come outside where the sun was shining.

"How am I doing?" she said. "That's a really great question. I think the answer would have to be pretty awful." She blew a loose strand of hair out of her eyes.

"Let's not wallow in all the stuff that went bad," I said. "Don't you think it would be better to look forward?"

"Yes," she said, a light finally coming to her eyes. "Let's not think about the past. Right, Lewis?"

"My sentiments exactly."

"Because, of course, the past had some pretty black moments, if you'd care to recall." I didn't like the tone in her voice. It was razor-edged with spite, and all of it was directed at me.

"Come on now," I said. "Where's the Sherise I used to know? We had some pretty great times."

She looked left and then right, as if she were scared someone nearby might be listening. Then, really quietly, almost in a whisper, she said, "Our child, Lewis."

Oh boy. I had been hoping this would not come up. Why do people always remember the bad things? When you let yourself get tangled up in all the ugly memories, that's when you get bogged down. That's when the past becomes a snare. And you'll never chew your way out of it.

"Our baby," she said. Her voice was rising. She was now talking a little louder than I would have liked.

"Please," I said. "Don't," I said.

"He was barely an hour old, Lewis. Remember?"

God damn that bitch. Seriously. Why did she have to go dredging up all that shit again? I was really hoping this would not happen.

"What we did was your idea, Lewis. And then you left. You left town and I haven't heard from you since." She bit at the side of her cheek for a few seconds. "So I'm sorry I'm not thinking about the 'great times.'"

She was hysterical, clearly. There would be no talking sense to her. There would be no coffee. No pleasant conversation or hitting the sheets for a quick tumble. No light-peck-on-the-cheek and see-you-around and let's-keep-in-touch. This whole reunion had gone straight to shit.

"Maybe I'd better leave," I said.

She nodded. "Yes. I think I would like that very much."

Sherise always knew how to cut a guy down. Chop, chop, chop and you were lying on the ground, dead and dying, ready for kindling.

I turned and left. There was nothing else for me to do. Don't try to tell me there was any sense in sticking around at that point. Because there wasn't.

Before leaving town, I got in touch with Tiny again. It was about four thirty in the afternoon and I had a hell of a drive ahead of me. Coffee and Mountain Dew weren't going to do the trick anymore.

I used some of the money from my windfall to score an eight ball. Tiny was cool about it. All business, no pleasantries—though I had already expected this, so it came as no great shock.

I hadn't done blow since I'd left LA, and the first toot was a real ass-kicker. Took me completely by surprise. But you get used to these things. They become second nature, after a while.

It's now going on midnight, and I'm still a few hours shy of Eureka. My plan thus far has been relatively snag-free, I'm happy to report. Though there will definitely be some explaining to do once I get back. My absence from work; the missing company truck; and the extra miles they're sure to find on the odometer in the morning. Those will require some smooth talking from old Trigger, no doubt. And, yes, the fact that there's no longer a rearview mirror on the truck. That'll raise some eyebrows. Frankly, I'm not sure yet what to tell them about that one—though the truth is simple enough. Because, see, just outside LA I got another screaming case of the Skeebers. Really bad this time. So I tore that rearview mirror off its bracket. I tore it right off and threw it out the window without stopping because I was afraid, if I looked in it, I might see my face.

3 Out of 5 Stars

This was the first vacuum I ever bought, so I didn't really know what I was looking for. I combed the aisle, pretending to make an informed decision, before settling on the Dynamex Life-Scrubber 3000. I hoisted the box off the shelf and solemnly proffered my plastic to the red-besmocked officiant at the cash register: a secular commitment ceremony.

Once I got the Life-Scrubber unboxed and assembled (iffy instructions, it should be noted), everything seemed fine. Those first few months were all about dust bunnies under the couch, cobwebs on the windowsills—small potatoes, cleaning-wise. You could say I was naïve to the types and depths of disorder that could infiltrate a person's life.

Three months later my girlfriend Janice had a living situation that had become untenable, and we decided it would be more tenable for her to move in with me. At that point things got harder for the Life-Scrubber 3000. It wasn't Janice who taxed the machine so much as it was her two Maine coons. (In case you're not familiar with that term, let me just say that they're a particular breed of cat. I'm also convinced they're somebody's idea of a sick joke. Maine coons weigh in around thirty pounds, and they're as friendly as bobcats.)

Janice called them Emma and Rosemary, but I privately referred to them as Butkus and C.H.U.D. Upon moving in, Butkus annexed the kitchen. I'd come home to find Cheerios or Kix littering the countertops and floors. For these messes, the Life-Scrubber's detachable extension hose made cleanups a snap.

C.H.U.D., on the other hand, took a keen interest in my houseplants, of which I used to have many. C.H.U.D. would methodically uproot and dismantle them, leaving their dismembered parts all over the living room. Potting soil was dug up and flung like blood spatter at a crime scene. While these messes were more of a nuisance than Butkus's kitchen adventures, they were still well within the Life-Scrubber's wheelhouse.

These early challenges were upsetting, but this was also back when things were still fresh between Janice and me. Back when we had the kind of sex that was so passionate, physical and raw that our bed smelled like a gladiator's locker room. It's easy to overlook the little things when you've got that going on. Of course, sex like that has a finite lifespan. Which turned out to be shorter than the Life-Scrubber's.

The biggest challenge, though, was the fur. My God, the fur! Another thing you may not know about Maine coons is that they are prolifically hirsute. They're covered in dense blooms of hair, which would accumulate in mounds of reddish fuzz. I'd do a pass-through with the Life-Scrubber, and within minutes, there'd be fresh piles waiting. If we opened a window to get some cross-ventilation going, waves of Maine coon fur would roll across the floors.

At this point I discovered the Life-Scrubber's limits. The roller brush began catching, which would cause the rubber belt to shriek and smoke. I disassembled it and found the brush clotted with hair. It took me forty minutes to clean and reassemble.

It was during one of the brush reassemblies that I recalled something on the original Life-Scrubber box. Amid the boilerplate, where it had informed unsuspecting consumers of its many features, had been the braggy slogan: "Designed to fit your lifestyle." That line now struck me as breathtakingly hubristic. What do these vacuum people know about my lifestyle? How could they claim to have designed a vacuum for it?

Then I got to thinking. What if the vacuum people were right, and the Life-Scrubber was indeed designed to fit my lifestyle? Maybe my current lifestyle was out of whack with its true nature. I began to contemplate why Janice and I were living together. The trials of cohabitation can make you lose sight of the fundamentals. What first drew me to Janice was her essential mysteriousness. In her Spotify library, she always gave her playlists names that were both cryptic and louche—*So Long Sly Stallone*; *Distant Macaroni Doodles*; *Hilltop Jesuit Empire*; *Kiss Me Marmalade Cousin*—like the dream journal entries of an opium addict. They'd made me feel like I could decode Janice, like I'd be a better person if (or when) I did.

But those goddamn Maine coons. They were a lifestyle no vacuum designer could have anticipated.

One Friday, while I was at the coffee shop, C.H.U.D. somehow forced an entry through the locked door to my office, which is where I kept several of my most prized possessions. Among those would be my aquarium containing a pair of not inexpensive Angelfish and one lovely Teardrop Butterflyfish.

I'd been gone less than an hour. By the time I returned, the massacre was over. C.H.U.D. was a thorough killer, and remorseless. My fish were scattered in ribbons around the office, julienned by C.H.U.D.'s sharp claws. And there he sat amid the carnage, licking bits of flesh from his whiskers. I chased C.H.U.D. around the apartment until Butkus came to his defense. Against one Maine coon, I believed I stood a chance. Against two, forget it.

I pulled out the Life-Scrubber, wheeled it to my office and began sucking up the remains, not caring that there was a warning in the user's guide against vacuuming wet items. I cleaned until I'd gathered every last scrap of fish, and then I did something awful.

I took the canister, full of still-wet fish pieces and Maine coon fur clumps, and emptied it on Janice's side of our bed in a *Godfather*-style display of dismembered animal parts. I then left the house and went to a bar down the street and proceeded to get blind drunk.

I don't know what Janice's immediate reaction was. I only know that she, Butkus, and C.H.U.D. were gone by the time I was coherent enough to remember anything. All that was left was a note asking me to be out of the apartment between 2 and 6 that next afternoon so her sister could collect the rest of her things.

I honored her request by going back to the bar down the street and getting slightly less blind drunk. That next day, I tried vacuuming up the remaining Maine coon fur, but the Life-Scrubber made a strange whining sound and emitted a reek of rotting fish. I tried finding a repair shop, but no one fixes vacuums anymore. So I carted the Life-Scrubber out to the alley, hoping that a flea picker might claim it. It was gone by the next morning.

So, bottom line: Is the Dynamex Life-Scrubber 3000 a decent vacuum? I suppose so. Can it handle garden-variety cleanups? Absolutely. But life will occasionally hand you big, all-encompassing messes—the kind that can bring you to your knees. What about those situations? It is any good for those? Don't kid yourself. It's only a vacuum.

Those Who Trespass

In the drawn-out silence between the second and third rings, Vincent Pease caught himself wishing his wife would not pick up the phone. He knew it was a bad sign to be harboring these thoughts at any point in a marriage, but particularly now.

The third ring sounded and he waited for the slight hitch that preceded the switch to voicemail.

"Hey—" Brenda's voice was breathless from a last-second dive for the phone.

"Hey yourself, darling," Vincent said, trying to strike the right mix of familiarity and formality these calls demanded.

"I'm sorry, honey, it's a little crazy around here." Brenda worked as a dental hygienist. Vincent took comfort in the fact that these mid-day calls were time-limited by her next appointment. "How's things with you?"

"Classes went well," he said. "Successfully molded more young minds."

"Listen, I've got a patient in the chair," she said, "but I wanted to see if we could do takeout tonight. Noodle Haus all right with you?"

"Noodles sound great," he said with conjured enthusiasm. "Want me to pick them up?"

"That'd be super," she said. "Oh yeah, Charlie and Donna invited us to dinner tomorrow night. That work for you?"

"Great, great," he said.

"You mind picking up a bottle of wine on the way home?"

"Are you forgetting you can't drink? Not for another seven months."

"The three of you can drink it. If you want I'll pick it up."

"I can handle it." Did his voice betray some annoyance there? He couldn't tell. "I'll stop by Castiglio's."

"Thanks, darling." She made some noises away from the receiver. "Gotta run."

When the call ended, his shoulders were drawn into knots, his jaw muscles so stiff they ached.

He stared at the computer screen for a few minutes, then rose and stepped into the hallway. As one of only three or four white faculty members at Carver Community College, Vincent knew he stuck out; he was used to it, and even relished the attention.

When he rounded the corner into the student bathroom, he was struck immediately by the incongruous sight of a red backpack slouching on the floor below one of the urinals.

He called out: "Is anyone here?"

His voice echoed off the concrete walls. So he gave a cursory look both ways and stepped up to the urinal next to the rumpled backpack. There was a small rip near its zipper. Several spots on the canvas were worn smooth with dirt.

God, he hated dinners with Charlie and Donna. They'd recently taken a wine-tasting course, and the two of them could go on for hours about the virtues of a particular bottle of Malbec. Eventually, they'd get around to asking Vincent a question about his job: "So what's it like working in…that neighborhood?"

He rinsed his hands and turned to leave, but his eye caught again on the backpack. Let it go, he said to himself. It's okay to let some things go.

≈

"You forgot the wine," Brenda said as she dropped the empty noodle cartons into the trash.

"What's that, honey?" Vincent had been watching a documentary about the economic crash in Venezuela, but he'd been unable to shake the image of that red backpack sitting beneath the urinal.

"You said you'd pick up the wine after work," she said. "For dinner with Charlie and Donna."

Brenda came to the doorway of the TV room and stood at the threshold. She'd recently adopted the habit of resting her right hand on the curve of her belly, though she was not yet showing.

His finger instinctively went to the mute button on the remote control. "Slipped my mind," he said. He hadn't told her about the backpack, which was now sitting in his office file cabinet.

"A little careless, don't you think?" A wedge of anger was working its way into her voice.

"I'm sorry, sweetie. Stressful day. You know how it is."

"No, I don't know," she said.

"What's that supposed to mean?"

"It means I have no idea what goes on down there. It—" She paused for a moment and seemed to be contemplating something. Her right hand traced small circles against her stomach. "Are you sleeping with one of your students?"

The rage Vincent felt at these words triggered a sudden coldness in his body. "There you go," he said. "Your stock accusation for every argument."

"It wasn't an accusation. It was a question."

"Give it a rest, Brenda. I don't hassle you when you've had a rough day."

"Fine." Her hand dropped lifelessly to her side. "I'll skip yoga and pick up the wine tomorrow." She waited for him to say something, but he refused to engage her further.

Eventually she slipped away from the door. He could hear her in the bathroom washing her face, removing her contacts, brushing her teeth. Vincent turned the sound up and tried to focus on the documentary—hordes of people ransacking empty grocery stores, turning over shelves and smashing windows; people fighting each other in the streets, their faces bloody and broken. Vincent thought: How could anyone, in good conscience, bring another human being into a world like this?

$$\approx$$

He had an hour between his first and second classes Friday morning, so he shut his office door and delicately unzipped the main compartment of the backpack.

Vincent knew he should just turn it in to lost and found, but he figured this way he might be able to track down the owner himself. I'm doing a good thing here, he thought. I'm doing someone a true kindness.

There were textbooks: Anatomy, Advanced Algebra, Sociology. He dug deeper and found a purple spiral notebook which he set on top of his desk. In the small back pocket he found a Ziploc baggie with three blunts. He pulled one out and caught the unmistakable whiff of cheap weed. He resealed the baggie and slipped it into the pocket of his overcoat.

He turned his attention to the purple spiral notebook. It contained entries written in a round, feminine script. Vincent hadn't before considered the possibility that this was a woman's backpack; the fact that it was found in a men's bathroom now seemed to hint at a deeper malevolence. Vincent struggled to control his breathing. The pads of his fingertips were sweating as he flipped through the pages.

It appeared to be a diary. The entries were focused on a boy named D'Kwan, whom the author had met while she was working her shift at McDonald's. D'Kwan had called her persistently for a few weeks until she'd finally given in and started seeing him. Their relationship was intensely physical, and her diary entries described their sex with an unashamed bluntness. But it was the strength of the writer's passion for D'Kwan that captivated Vincent. And as he picked up on the first inklings of the relationship's demise—an argument here, an unreturned phone call there—he felt his own stomach start to turn. The final entry detailed the unhappy conclusion.

> D'Kwan left, he say I don't do nothing for him no more and he going back to his old girl. I try to say to him I love him and wont to be with him but, he say Im no good for him. Maybe he right, I don't know. Something says he right I tell him Im carrying his child, but he know thats a ly. And I fill a fool for even saying it to him when what I wont to say is I wont to have his baby. But he gone now and there aint no help for me in this world.

To Vincent, it was a bleak symphony of despair played out in the silence of his office.

As he moved to close the notebook, a white piece of paper slipped onto his lap. It was a pay stub in the amount of $263.67 from McDonald's, for a person named Latricsa Williams.

The phone on Vincent's desk let out a jarring ring, and he dropped the notebook onto the floor.

"My ten o'clock canceled, so I'm at the store looking at wine right now." Brenda's voice was light and breezy. He could tell she was trying to gloss over last night's squabble.

"I'm really sorry, honey," he said, retrieving the notebook and slipping the pay stub back into it.

"It's fine, darling. I was just calling to get a recommendation."

He hated picking out wine for Charlie and Donna. No matter what he brought, they'd take a long look at the bottle and say it sounded good, but they had something else that might go a little better with dinner. "Does it really matter?" he asked.

"Of course it matters. I want them to enjoy the gift we're bringing."

"Listen, honey, I've got a student here for a conference. I trust your judgment."

When he hung up, he slid the purple notebook into the backpack and left for his next class.

≈

The sign below the golden arches indicated that this was a "Hip Hop" McDonald's—a fact which Vincent found to be immensely condescending. It was the only restaurant within walking distance of Carver, but he'd never set foot inside it before. The only difference, as far as he could tell, between a regular McDonald's and a Hip Hop McDonald's was that this one had a faux-Egyptian statue near the seating area, and black-and-white photos of various rap stars on the walls.

Off campus, he felt like he was penetrating deeper into the heart of something unknown, and the backpack was a talisman that would grant him safe passage. He carried it prominently on his shoulder, reminding himself that his intentions were noble. He went up to the counter and a skinny girl with short braids asked to take his order.

He had been hoping that Latricsa might be working today, that she'd notice the backpack and claim it. But everyone behind the counter was busy filling orders, so he placed his, and took a seat in view of the counter.

He lay the backpack on the table across from him and set about eating his food. It was the early side of the lunch rush and a steady stream of customers trickled in. They glanced at him, some of them doing stifled double-takes, but no one said a word. According to the diary, Latricsa was left by herself to close one night. She was just locking up the tills when D'Kwan stopped by to pick her up. She let him in, even though he was drunk. And eventually he took her from behind in one of the booths, her face pressed up against the cold window glass. Vincent recalled a line from that entry: *D'Kwan like to fuck raw and he always nut in me, even though I know it aint safe.* Vincent's gaze wandered slowly around the restaurant, trying to imagine which booth they'd used.

"Hey, look! Professor Peabody."

Vincent was yanked from his reverie. He knew Professor Peabody was the nickname some of the students used for him, a well-meaning-enough dig. Vincent looked up and recognized the face of a kid named Nashid Shepherd. He'd been a standout student in Vincent's freshman comp last fall. He'd written his final research paper on the societal effects of mass incarceration; Vincent had found it truly eye-opening. He was relieved to see his former student's smiling face here today.

"Hey, Nashid," he said. "How you getting along this semester?"

"Keeping straight," Nashid said, shrugging his shoulders. "You know."

"Good, good." There was an awkward pause while Vincent tried to think of something else to say.

"What're you doing so far from campus?" Nashid asked.

"Carver's only two blocks away. Am I that far off my turf?"

Nashid looked around, as if he were suddenly embarrassed to be having this conversation. "You know, professors don't like to get off campus too much up in here."

"I'm trying to explore a little. Broaden my horizons."

"Right," Nashid giggled. "Like some kinda tourist."

"I guess so."

"All right then. Enjoy the horizons, professor." They shook hands formally, and Nashid sauntered off to the far side of the dining area.

When Vincent had finished his food, he went up to the counter and the same skinny girl with short braids asked him if he wanted anything else.

"Can I speak with the manager, please?" he asked in a quiet voice.

"That's me," she said defensively. She tapped the plastic tag on her shirt. Below the name Sheronda, it said Manager.

"Oh, sorry," he said. "I'm trying to locate someone named Latricsa Williams?"

The girl glared at him and bit her lower lip. She had a tiny gold stud in her left nostril.

"Does she work here?" he asked.

"Not no more." The girl wiped her hands on her apron. "Not for two weeks."

"Do you have any idea where she might be?"

The girl gave him a sidelong glance. "Why you looking for her?"

Vincent paused a moment, unsure what to say. "Thanks anyway," he said. "Sorry I bothered you."

≈

By the time he got back to his office, Vincent was keyed up. The mystery surrounding the backpack had only grown deeper. And it was up to him to solve it.

His fingers fluttered as he clicked on the Student Records icon on his computer desktop and entered his password. He typed in *Williams, Latricsa* and pulled up her academic file. She'd been enrolled at Carver for a year and a half. Judging by the classes she'd taken, she was majoring in nursing. Her grades had been mostly Bs and Cs, with a smattering of Incompletes. She was enrolled this semester in the three courses that corresponded with the textbooks in the backpack.

He clicked on Personal Information and her phone number popped up. He glanced at the phone on his desk. A siren went by on the street outside. He lifted the receiver and dialed the number. The phone rang twice and then picked up. He inhaled, ready to speak, but his ear was jangled by the three minor notes of the disconnect recording.

Vincent's eyes cut back to the computer screen. He scrolled down to her home address.

≈

It was dark by the time Vincent pulled up to the address. He saw a set of gates with a sign saying Margaret Henson Housing Project. Henson House—the largest public housing project on this side of town. He'd often heard his students talking about it, and it was frequently mentioned on the local news, but he'd never actually seen it before.

There was no parking along the front, so he pulled around to a side street and wedged his Camry between a beat-up Cutlass and a showroom-quality Escalade. His heart was beating wildly in his chest; his hands were shaking. He reached into the pocket of his overcoat, felt the plastic baggie of blunts, and removed one. The wrapping leaves were brittle as he turned it over in his unsteady hands. He looked around outside the car. The houses here were dark. The streets were empty.

He pushed the cigarette lighter in. When it popped out, he held the cigar to his mouth and delicately touched the tip against the glowing hot metal. He inhaled once, twice. The smoke was dry and acrid and burned his throat. He hadn't smoked weed since grad school. He coughed roughly, pushing the smoke out of his lungs and clouding the cramped interior of the car.

His phone rang, and he looked around guiltily. He unrolled his window and dropped the half-smoked cigar into the gutter.

"Where are you, honey?" Brenda asked. "You didn't call this afternoon. I was worried."

"I'm fine, darling. Things got hectic. Lots of student conferences."

"I just finished yoga," she said, then paused, waiting for him to ask her about it. "Are you almost home?" she asked when it was clear he wasn't going to respond.

"Not quite," he said, glancing at the dashboard clock: 5:45.

"Dinner's at 6:30, darling. You know how anal Charlie and Donna are about time."

"I might be a little late."

"How late?"

"I'm running a few errands, honey."

"Your voice sounds funny."

"Nothing," he said. "I don't know."

"What's wrong with you?"

He hung up the phone and shoved it into the glove box.

Finally he shut off the ignition and climbed out of the Camry. As he rounded the corner, he saw three teenage boys—none of them more than fifteen years old—hanging out near the bus stop. They were play-fighting with each other, which, to Vincent, looked a lot like actual fighting. Despite the cold, one of the boys wore a loose-fitting Hawaiian shirt with a bright red floral print. He had a soft-serve ice cream cone in one hand that the other two boys were trying to knock over. They froze when they saw Vincent. All three were smaller than him, but the hardness etched into their faces made them seem powerful. Vincent knew turning back now would only invite trouble.

I'm a good guy, he reminded himself. I'm returning someone's lost property. But the words rang hollow in his mind as he walked past the staring boys, clutching the backpack strap firmly in his hand.

Though he knew he should feel guilty about it, he perceptibly picked up his walking pace. He turned the corner into Henson House.

The courtyard was long and narrow and dark. The shrubs that served as landscaping were brown, dead. The grass was strewn with fast food wrappers and plastic bottles. Nothing here could biodegrade any further.

It took him a few seconds to figure out the numbering system, and by the time he did, he thought he could hear the kids from the bus stop following him. The first thing he imagined he would feel was the ice cream cone splattering against the back of his head, running down his neck as it melted against his skin. Then the real blows would come. He had nothing to defend himself with but the awkward weight of the backpack. When he turned around, though, he saw no one behind him. Still, he wasn't reassured.

Vincent found a screened-in metal staircase that looked like it belonged in a prison. He began vaulting up the stairs two at a time, to make it look like he had a purpose.

The windows along the outer walkway were covered in bars, and the doors to the apartments were stout, with nothing other than numbers indicating who might be inside.

Vincent walked down to the number he'd written on the sticky note. He knocked, waited thirty seconds and knocked again. He looked around and realized he was engulfed by the housing project. Every direction he looked, he saw low, bunker-like buildings with tiny windows—a universe of concrete. He knocked one more time and began to brace himself for the walk back to his car.

Then the door opened a few inches. A chain lock stretched across the dark span.

"Who you with?" a woman's voice called out. Her face was hidden behind the door.

"I'm not with anyone," he said. Then, "I'm an English professor at Carver Community College."

"What you want?" She wasn't trying to hide the distrust in her voice.

"I'm trying to find Latricsa Williams."

"She don't live here no more," the woman snapped.

"Do you know where she is? I'm trying to return something that belongs to her."

"Only the Lord know where she at."

"I have her backpack." He took the pack from his shoulder and offered it to the dark crack of the door. "I found it at Carver. In one of the bathrooms."

There was a long pause. The door closed. Vincent could hear the chain lock sliding off its hook. The door opened again and the voice said, "You might as well come in."

Vincent stepped carefully into the room. The blinds were closed and no lights were on and he couldn't make out anything in the room.

"Close the door behind you and fix the lock." The voice was coming from somewhere deeper in the room. Vincent turned around and did what she'd asked.

"Take a seat."

He stumbled around until he found a recliner. It was low, with a soft cushion, and he felt himself sinking deeply into it. He rested the backpack on his lap, the heavy textbooks digging into his thighs. It was warm in the apartment and as the heat hit his bones, he realized how cold his body had been—cold right down to the core. Slowly, his eyes began to adjust to the darkness.

He was in a living room. The white walls were adorned with framed posters of nature scenes—a tropical rainforest, a palm-covered beach, a snow-capped mountain—places almost preposterous in their postcard beauty, and so far removed from their present location as to be more like figments of a fertile imagination.

The woman who spoke to him was sitting on a couch across the room. She wore a purple bathrobe, and was enormously fat. The couch cushions flexed under her weight and stuck up at the corners. There was a coffee table between them. On it was a single burning candle in a jar that gave off a sweet vanilla smell.

"She always wanted to travel," the woman said, waving a hand around the room. "These were her pictures."

Vincent nodded approvingly. He felt like it was an act of fate that had brought the two of them here, to this room. Yet words, the proper response, eluded him.

The woman curled her legs onto the couch. Vincent could still feel the heat of the room penetrating him, filling him up. He was sweating, but didn't know if he could ever feel warm enough.

"She gone now," the woman said, almost mumbling.

"Gone where?"

The woman shook her head. "The streets," she said. "The streets took her."

Vincent had an image of a giant pothole opening up and swallowing a girl whole. "Will she be back, do you think?"

"Maybe," the woman said. "Maybe not. Two weeks ago, she don't come back from school when she supposed to. I ain't heard nothing from her and no one else has neither."

Vincent shifted the backpack on his lap.

"Guess I should offer you something to eat or drink, but I don't got nothing to give you right now."

"I'm all right," he said. His voice was scratchy and raw from the blunt.

"That her backpack?"

"I think so."

She grunted and leaned hard against the armrest. A spring somewhere in the couch buckled.

Vincent couldn't tell if she wanted him to leave. He felt like a parasite, drinking in something he needed in a place where he wasn't wanted.

"Latricsa was a good student," he lied. "I was always glad to see her in class."

The woman cast a skeptical glance at him. "How's that?"

"She was always very thoughtful," he said. "Very…nice." He hated the way this sounded. "She never spoke much in class, but I always got the impression there was a lot going on with her. Lots of thoughts and ideas and, well," he stammered, struggled with the words in his head. He thought about the journal he'd read, and about that last entry. "She had the soul of a poet."

The woman smiled. It was an easy smile that gave her face a certain beauty. "She did, huh? My baby girl?"

Vincent nodded deeply. "Yes."

"Do you have a child, mister?"

The question caught Vincent off guard. He said, "My students are my children."

The woman appeared to be contemplating this thought for a moment. Then her smile faded. "And what class you say you teach my Tricsa?"

"I'm an English teacher."

"She wasn't taking no English class this semester."

Vincent's throat went tight. He hadn't expected this level of scrutiny. "Anyway," he said, trying to cover, "I found the backpack in one of the school bathrooms. I asked at the McDonald's, but they said they hadn't seen her."

The woman's face narrowed further. "How you know she work at McDonald's?"

His mind was spinning, trying desperately to find a plausible explanation. "Well, now, that's—"

"What's this mess going on here?" The woman's voice shattered the quiet of the dark apartment. "You playing some kind of game?"

"No, I'm not."

"You know where my baby at?"

"No. I don't. I'm just a good Samaritan trying to return a lost backpack." He held his empty hands out before him.

"Tell me where she at. Tell me, mister, so help me God."

"I have no idea where your daughter is. I wish I could be more help, but I can't."

The woman rose from the couch. "You come into my house smelling like weed, and you got her bag, and you ain't even her teacher? Uh-uh. No way." Her feet were placed squarely on the floor, her hands balled into fists. "You don't got no business here. And if you do, ain't none of it good."

"I'm sorry, ma'am. I didn't mean to intrude, but—"

"I want you out my house right now."

"But—"

The woman took a deep breath. "Turn around and walk out my house or I'm calling the police."

There was nothing more he could do or say. He set the backpack on the floor and went to the entryway. The woman followed him, and when he stepped out into the cold, she slammed the door so hard it rattled on its hinges. A second later he heard the chain lock slide into place.

As the cold air seeped back into his bones, he realized it wasn't kindness or altruism that had brought him to this point. It was something else, a hunger that had gone unsatisfied.

Vincent looked out over the edge of the railing. Did he hear voices? He didn't think so, but he couldn't be sure. There was no way to tell what awaited him below, what awaited him at home. He looked at the locked door behind him, and he looked at the stairwell, and he knew the only direction he could go was down.

Ling

Chuck's mother was beached on the living room couch. Her black hair was a tangled mess of seaweed draped across her face. She wasn't dead, but Sammy only knew this because he could see her ribcage rising and falling. On the coffee table, a half dozen plastic cups. In the air, the scent of gin and menthols. The television was blaring some cop show.

Sammy didn't know what to do. Why would Chuck's sister leave him here to see this? When did the Lawrys become the kind of family where this was normal?

Sammy steeled himself and perched on the edge of a recliner. He tried to focus on the TV. A cop said to a criminal, "Did you really think you'd get away with it? Did you? Really?"

Sammy listened for noise from the back of the house, some sign that Chuck was almost ready and would come out so they could leave. If he held his breath and listened hard, he thought he could hear squabbling voices, but he couldn't make out the words.

Mrs. Lawry murmured and shifted. Her arm flopped off the couch, fingertips grazing the carpet. As Sammy looked on, he realized that this new position had parted the top of her blouse and exposed her left breast.

Her skin was the color of notebook paper. Underneath it, he could see a delicate webbing of veins. Her nipple was cotton candy pink. Sammy forced himself to look back at the TV. A shootout was going on, but no one was hitting who they were aiming at.

Mrs. Lawry began snoring. It was a loud, almost painful rasp that sounded like it was going to stop at any moment. People died like this. Sammy could no longer avert his eyes. He knew he should do something, but didn't know what.

"Christ, Mom!" It was Chuck, finally emerged from the back of the house. "You look like a goddamn mess."

Hearing her son's voice, Mrs. Lawry's eyes fluttered open. She looked around the room, then casually tucked her breast into her blouse and went back to sleep.

"You ready?" Chuck asked Sammy.

Sammy's face was hot. He wasn't sure what to do—if he should apologize for what he'd seen, or pretend it never happened.

"Let's go," Chuck said.

Out in the garage, Sammy popped the tailgate of the Lawrys' Citation. He brushed aside a pile of balled-up fast food wrappers and loaded his rod and tackle box. Meanwhile, Chuck lifted a twelve-pack of Stroh's from the garage fridge. He placed it in a cooler which he set next to the fishing gear. When they got into the car, Sammy noticed Chuck's hair was wet-combed and he smelled like soap.

"You took a shower?" Sammy asked.

"I invited Candace," Chuck said, craning his neck as he backed the car out of the garage. "She might join up with us later."

Chuck and Candace had been dating for six months. She had frosted blond hair and usually wore tight pocketless

Wranglers. She was attractive in a way that would not last long. But for now she was easily one of the prettiest girls at Roosevelt High.

"You don't mind, do you?" Chuck asked.

"If you want to invite your girlfriend fishing, it's not my problem." Sammy tried to sound flip.

"Maybe if you got yourself a girlfriend you could invite her too."

"Yeah right," Sammy said. "And watch her faint at the first sight of a ling."

"I'm more worried about *you* fainting," Chuck said. He threw the gearshift into drive, and the transmission caught a second later.

They each cracked a beer and kept it nestled between their thighs. Sammy wanted to say something about what had happened in the living room.

"Is everything all right?" he tried. "At home?"

"What do you think?" Chuck snapped.

Heading east on 4th Avenue, past the car dealerships and truck repair shops, the stoplights were timed. As they came to each one, Chuck kept his foot on the gas, confident the lights would keep turning green and they'd shoot through each intersection unscathed.

≈

Sammy had gotten used to feeling like the future was never going to arrive—doomed to perpetually recede, like that part of the highway that always looks wet on the horizon. But now that he was a senior in high school, it seemed at long last like it was taking shape before him. He'd go away to college next fall, reinvent himself, correct the things he'd gotten wrong. The first eighteen years hadn't been a disaster, even if there were things about himself he'd gladly kill if he had the chance.

They'd both finished their first beer by the time Chuck nosed the Citation into a spot along the river. The juniper scrub was thick, and the car was nearly invisible. Sammy wondered how Candace was supposed to find them here.

The bank was a steep five-foot drop that curved out at the bottom to provide a flat beach where they could set up their equipment, the cooler, firewood. The Yellowstone's water was impenetrably dark. Eddies formed and made sucking sounds, hinting at a depth that Sammy found frightening. Every year someone died along this stretch of the river. Inner-tubers, drunken rafters, careless people who didn't understand its power.

Sammy began pulling up rocks and setting them in a circle. Chuck arranged kindling in a tepee formation.

"Fire's the key," Chuck said, as he stuffed a wad of newspaper underneath the sticks. "Ling are attracted to the light. Makes them hungry, ready to feed on the first thing they see." He held a match to the newspapers and it caught, releasing an inky smoke into the night sky.

Growing up, Sammy had had little exposure to the kinds of outdoor survival activities that were the currency of manhood in Montana. Chuck was more of an expert. He was the one who'd suggested they go ling fishing. Sammy had never even heard of ling before that. And all he knew about them now was the little Chuck had told him: they were a long, snake-like fish, and their meat was considered a delicacy, flaky as French pastry.

"Let's rig up," Chuck said. He flipped open the cooler, removed a plastic freezer bag, and held it up to the light. To Sammy it looked like leeches, gorged on fresh blood.

"Christ, what is that?"

"Chicken livers." Chuck's voice sounded cheerfully efficient. "I let them age a few days at room temperature. Should be nice and pungent."

He pulled the zip-seal open. Sammy caught a whiff and had to stifle a gag in the back of his throat. Chuck let out a cackling laugh.

"I'm not touching those things," Sammy said. He didn't care how weak or prissy he sounded.

"Maybe I let them get a little too ripe," Chuck admitted. "Entirely possible."

"Here's my hook," Sammy said, feeding line from his reel. "You put one on."

Chuck shook his head, but eventually squatted next to the dangling line. He reached into the bag and pulled one out. His face was set in a stony frown as he pierced and re-pierced it onto the hook. Occasionally, the smell would overwhelm him and he'd turn his head to the side to steal a breath of clean air.

Once Chuck had both hooks baited, they squeezed lead weights onto the lines. Then they gingerly heaved their rigs as far out as they could into the current. Sammy had a nervous feeling in his stomach, a feeling he got every time he went fishing. It was the anxiety of being tethered to something primitive and unknown.

They arranged piles of anchor rocks and propped their rods so they rested at forty-five degree angles, tips out over the water, monofilament lines disappearing into the dark.

"So that's it, then." Sammy wondered if he meant it as a question. He cracked a beer and took a long slug. As he pulled the can down, he noticed his hands were shaking.

"I imagine so." Chuck stamped his feet on the rocks to keep warm.

A plane descending for the airport north of town cast a roar that came on fast and faded slowly into the distance. The water before them did not reflect the canopy of star- and moonlight. It swirled and sucked like a thirsty drain gulping water.

≈

"Do you really think we'll do it?" Chuck asked. His face was shadowed, brooding. By now they'd drunk enough beer that words came more freely.

"Do what?" Sammy was sitting on a rock close to the fire.

"Go to war. Take out Saddam once and for all."

"They'd be crazy to tempt us." Sammy glanced at the rod tips, slightly bent from the tug of the current. "They'll probably let the inspectors in at the last minute."

"Yeah, but that shithead just wants everything his way."

Sammy wasn't sure who his friend thought was the shithead. "I do worry if things go bad, it could become a long-term thing."

"Long-term thing," Chuck echoed. His voice sounded distant, distracted, as if his mind had already moved on.

"Yeah, it could become another Vietnam. They could start a draft." Sammy was parroting something he'd heard on TV the other day, even though he didn't really believe it. When he actually watched the coverage, he regarded it all with a sense of distant curiosity, the way you might observe footage of a bad storm that had hit a neighborhood where you used to live.

Chuck didn't say anything for a long time. He tossed an empty can on the fire and watched it. Finally he said, "Do you ever wonder what it'd be like to live under water?"

Sammy was thrown by the sudden change in subject.

"You know," Chuck said, "if you were a fish. What would it be like?"

"I'm not a good swimmer."

Chuck didn't crack a smile. "Scary, then," he said, frustrated. "Just say it would be scary."

Sammy took a drink of beer. He looked again at the rod tips.

"You heard from any schools yet?" Chuck asked.

"Too early," Sammy said. "Not until April."

A breeze kicked up, riffling the water and shaking the branches of the cottonwoods nearby so they squeaked like rusty hinges.

"Don't you want to know if I heard from any schools?" Chuck asked.

"I thought you said you weren't applying anywhere."

"Relax, I'm not. I was just kidding."

"Maybe getting out of your house would be a good thing for you," Sammy suggested.

"Ha! You think?"

"I'm serious. A change of scenery could only help."

Chuck leaned back against a rock and kicked his feet out, soles facing the fire.

"I know it's none of my business," Sammy said. "Sorry."

Chuck crossed his legs and let out a long sigh. "Hell," he said, "maybe a draft would be a great thing for someone like me."

The can he'd thrown into the fire was warping now, giving in to some elemental form. Very soon, it would be indistinguishable from everything else around it.

≈

Sammy pushed up his coat sleeve and saw that it was 11:45. His legs were stiff and cold; he couldn't feel his feet. They were down to the last piece of firewood.

Throughout the night they'd periodically reel in their lines to find that something had slipped the bait from their hooks.

"You think it's a ling?" Sammy asked.

"Probably just the current," Chuck said. "Make sure you put it on good."

Sammy was drunk enough now that he didn't mind handling the foul livers. Just one more item he could add to his list of disgusting outdoor things he'd done.

"Hey, Chuck," he said, holding his hand out toward him. "Smell my finger."

"Fuck off," Chuck said, batting his hand away.

They both laughed for a few seconds and then it grew quiet and the only sounds came from the river.

"So is Candace coming?" Sammy asked, trying to make it sound like idle curiosity.

"Who cares," Chuck said.

As the night had worn on, Chuck had become more and more restless. He'd taken to pacing up and down the shoreline, staring at the water as if he hoped to see through it to the bottom. He'd hurled his last two empty cans into the river. As Sammy watched him, he could foresee the ways Chuck would age—a thickening around the paunch, a filling out around the jowls, a retreat of the hairline. Sammy wondered if his own destiny was as easily discernible.

"Goddamn, where are all those ling?" Chuck shouted at the water.

"What did she say she was doing tonight?"

"Who?"

"Candace."

"Out with friends," Chuck said, more to the river than to Sammy.

"So she might not meet us then?"

Chuck turned. "You figured it out. Bravo, asshole."

Sammy shifted on the rock. He'd exposed his thoughts in a way he hadn't intended. "Dude," he said, trying to slur his words, "I'm definitely wasted."

Chuck shook his head. "I know you want to bang my girlfriend."

Sammy opened his mouth, unsure what would come out.

"You can pretend all innocent if you want," Chuck said, "but I can see right through you. It's pretty fucking obvious."

Sammy knew he had to say something, either to save face or smooth things over. But in the space where his words should have been, he heard a scratching sound. He looked past Chuck and saw one of the fishing rods flexing.

Chuck followed Sammy's gaze. They were both frozen for a moment as the rod tip danced and darted, and the anchor rocks began to shift. Then they scrambled. Chuck got to it first. He gave the rod a sharp snap back to set the hook.

"Get the net, get the net," he said to Sammy.

The reel gave out a high-pitched whine as the tension pulled on the spool. But Chuck was good. He knew how to play a fish—even a fish deep in the current, as this one clearly was; even a big fish, as this one seemed like it might be.

He repeatedly raised the rod tip over his head and then reeled furiously as he lowered it back down. The line steadily shortened.

Sammy gripped the net. He could feel his pulse pounding in his temples as he watched the line slice left, then right, through the water.

Dimly at first, he caught sight of it—a wavy slick of motor oil. Then it rose and broke the surface and he saw that it had actual substance.

"Net, net, net!" Chuck called out over the screams of his over-taxed reel. "Go, go, go!"

Sammy leaned out and sank the net mouth below the fish. Then with a swoop of his arms, he delivered the fish into the night air.

It looked like it was made of some alien substance that might split into pieces, slip through the netting and reassemble itself in the water. Chuck tossed the rod aside and moved in. He grabbed the fish below the gills and worked the hook from its lip. When he pulled it out of the net, they could see it was as long as Chuck's arm, and twice as thick around. Black with greenish spots, it looked more like a snake than a fish: prehistoric, not fully evolved.

Its slimy tail flailed wildly for a few seconds, then coiled around Chuck's forearm.

"Christ, it's disgusting!" he shouted. "Get a rock!"

All at once, Sammy realized what they'd come here to do. Before this moment it had only been theoretical. His body went sluggish; his feet were impossibly heavy.

"What are you waiting for?" Chuck screamed. "Get a rock!"

The fish's gills flexed and bellowed, struggling vainly against the unfamiliar air.

"*You* get a rock," Sammy said, his voice quiet and low.

"Look at this thing, dumbass! It's on my goddamn arm."

"You get a rock," Sammy said again, louder. "I'm not going to be the one to kill it."

Chuck huffed. "Grab it, then." He held his arm out.

Sammy pinched the fish just below the gills. When he squeezed, the flesh felt like bread dough. He tugged until the tail uncoiled itself from Chuck's arm and began waving about for something else to latch onto.

The skin was coated with a thick slime. And the muscles in the fish's neck pulsed beneath Sammy's fingers. Its face was ugly—big mouth, craggy teeth, eyes bulging. The tail was twisting into a corkscrew now, grasping itself.

Chuck came back carrying a large flat rock in both hands.

"Hold it over there," he said, "and I'll bash it."

Sammy hesitated.

"Come on. Do it."

Sammy started to turn, but even as he did so, he felt his grip weaken. The fish unwound its tail and began thrashing with a renewed force.

"Get a hold of it, Sammy. Bring it here."

But it was too late. The head slipped through his grasp. The fish landed hard on the beach and rolled over. Bits of sand and twigs stuck to its sides.

Chuck pounced, but with one last thrash, the fish was able to heave itself back into the shallows. It sat there a moment, shedding its terrestrial debris, refilling its cold fish blood with oxygen. Chuck recovered and ran into the water, chasing it, but by the time he got there, the fish gave a few wriggles and turned back into oil.

Chuck, knee deep in the frigid water, slapped the surface. "What the hell was that?"

Sammy held his hands out at his sides. "It slipped."

Chuck squared his shoulders, hands balled into fists. "The fuck it did." His eyes were two narrow slits.

"Come on, man. It happened."

"Do you have any idea what you did?" As his friend came closer, Sammy could see tears streaming from the corners of his eyes. His bottom lip was quivering.

"Are you crying?"

Chuck kept coming, chest out, fist cocked. "You ruined it."

"Ruined what?" he asked.

Headlight beams appeared over the bank above them. Chuck stopped advancing. They heard the sounds of someone making their way through the brush near the bank. Both boys turned. Sammy figured Candace was coming after all, arriving in the nick of time—either to save him or to bear witness to his humiliation.

Chuck, staring up at the light, said: "Mom, is that you?"

Sammy couldn't believe it. Those had to be the saddest four words he'd ever heard. He looked at Chuck, saw the irrational, childlike hope in his friend's eyes. And right then the thought flared in Sammy's mind that he would probably go his whole life without really understanding another human being.

More noise from above. Then a police officer materialized at the edge of the bank and looked down at them—hands at his hips, bulky gun reflected in the headlights.

"Saw some light coming from back in here," he said. "What's going on, boys?"

Chuck and Sammy exchanged glances. Both of them were too surprised to speak.

"Is that fishing tackle?" The cop seemed old to Sammy, maybe in his mid-fifties.

"Yes, sir," Sammy managed.

"You boys linging?"

They both said yes at the same time.

"There's no ling around here this time of year. You've been wasting your time." The walkie-talkie clipped to his shoulder gave out a pop and a hiss. "Awful lot of stray cans down there. You been drinking?"

"Just a few beers, officer," Sammy said because it seemed pointless to try and cover it up.

"If you've been out here all night, you must be frozen." The cop looked up at the headlight beams as they illuminated a path across the river. He seemed to be thinking. "I suppose in some way that's punishment enough. Why don't you boys just pull your crap together? Pack up and get the hell out of here. We'll call this a warning."

≈

They were both silent as Chuck drove back into town. Sammy was trying to figure out why the cop had let them go. What exactly had he seen as he looked down on them from the bank? This question seemed important to Sammy, but the more he thought about it, the further he was from an answer.

In the driver's seat, Chuck gripped the steering wheel hard with both hands. He too was lost in thought. Sammy knew Chuck would tell people at school what had happened with the fish, that Sammy had gotten freaked out, that he couldn't hold onto the ling for even a few seconds. Sammy knew there would be ridicule coming his way.

But this was of little concern to him as the Citation navigated the empty streets. He'd be graduating in a few short months. Off to college—new city, new friends, everything new—and he would reshape the story to make himself seem less culpable, more heroic.

The Citation pulled up in front of Sammy's house.

"All right then," Sammy said.

Chuck was silent.

"I'll see you later."

Sammy got out. Chuck pulled away. The air felt cold on Sammy's face. But he stood there motionless, watching the car recede until the taillights were red pinpricks in the night. As soon as they disappeared, he knew, something would be gone for good.

Homefront

At 10:17 AM Monty got the call informing him that his mother had died sometime the day before. She'd passed away in the home. Luckily, a worried neighbor had called in an anonymous wellness check. Otherwise…well, Monty didn't want to think about otherwise. He'd always known this day would come, that he'd be compelled to go back. Better to do it quickly, he thought. One last clean break.

Maura wanted him to wait, at least until their son's fever broke. They argued about it. One of those trench warfare fights they'd been having lately where they were both so dug in neither of them seemed to have a way of communicating, much less surrendering. When it was over, he booked the next available flight. That afternoon, looking down on the clouds as his plane climbed away from Chicago, Monty realized what he'd been unable to tell Maura: He needed to go back alone.

≈

The old phone in his mother's kitchen let out a grinding ring that shattered the quiet of the empty house. Monty stared at it. He felt vulnerable, an intruder caught behind enemy lines.

"Jesus, Monty, where have you been?" It was Maura. "Your phone's going straight to voicemail."

He could hear a faint cry on the other end. Sounded like Dillon—just part of the white noise that permeated their daily existence.

"Is everything okay with Dillon?" he asked.

"Same. Fever hasn't broken."

"And the doctor?"

"Said to wait."

The line was quiet. All essential information had been exchanged.

"I must've forgotten to turn my phone on after the plane," he said. "Sorry."

There was a slight pause in Dillon's crying. Maura asked, "What's it like being back?"

"Pretty depressing so far." There was more he could say but didn't, perhaps to protect her from the true darkness of his mood.

"Any regrets?"

Monty wasn't sure if she was fishing for an apology. "Of course," he said. "I have regrets about almost everything." He could hear how bad this sounded as soon as the words left his mouth, so he added, "I wish you could be here."

This last line was bait, he supposed, to let Maura reignite their earlier argument. She sighed instead, a semaphore of resignation.

"Forget it," he said. "Let me know if things change with Dillon."

"Keep your phone on," she said. "I can't believe I still had your mom's number in my contacts."

When he hung up, the house fell silent. It was dark outside, only a fraction brighter inside. His two main responsibilities were arranging some kind of memorial service for his mother, and settling the estate. Both tasks would be easier to accomplish if he could get a hold of his brother Simon. There'd been no answer when he'd tried reaching him earlier. It would be just like Simon to dodge this final obligation.

Monty opened his cell phone and pulled up the most recent number he had for his brother. Instead of hitting send, though, Monty decided to dial from his mother's phone. Between the first and second rings someone picked up.

"I'm trying to reach Simon Creel," he said.

"Are you joking?" The voice belonged to a woman—young, sullen.

"This is the last number I have for him," Monty said. "Simon's my brother. Our mother just died."

"This isn't his number anymore." Her voice was harder now, as if the fact that their mother was dead had made her less sympathetic.

"Do you know where I can reach him?" Monty asked, but she'd already hung up.

≈

It was 6:45 AM when he awoke. It had been a restless sleep. At one point, on the edge of consciousness, he could have sworn he'd heard footsteps, the same sound his father used to make when he'd stagger down the hallway at night. But now Monty wasn't sure if it had been a dream. Ghosts, he knew, were nothing more than powerful memories. And there were plenty of those to go around.

He went through the house opening shades and windows. The estate sale people would arrive in a couple hours. This was a little rushed, a breach of etiquette perhaps, but he wasn't about to stand on ceremony.

His mother hadn't done much to keep things up the last couple years. Stacks of newspapers circling the dining room, mugs with dried rings of coffee measuring daily evaporation rates. The sorry sight of it would have induced a better man to feel guilty, but it just made Monty lonely. He tried calling Maura. He wanted to tell her that nothing from the past, neither these rooms nor his memories of them, seemed like they were the right size anymore. The phone rolled over to voicemail so he hung up.

He found some cleaning supplies under the sink, then turned on the kitchen radio. The work was gratifying. The ammonia fumes scalded his nostrils as bucket after bucket became cloudy, then brown, from years of accumulated dirt. He was bringing this house back to an earlier time.

As he was running a vacuum through the bedroom he'd shared with Simon, a nostalgic memory came back. He knelt down, counted ten floorboards from the foot of the bunk beds, and knocked until he found a hollow spot. Using his thumbnail, he pried up the loose board to find the cubbyhole where he'd kept his adolescent stash of *Playboys* and *Penthouses*. They were gone. In their place, he found a Ziploc bag.

Monty picked it up, held it to the light. A couple joints, some white pills, several folded squares of foil, and a key that looked like it might fit a bus station locker. Fucking Simon. Monty shoved the bag into his pocket. He heard his cell phone ring back in the living room but it stopped by the time he got there. Maura. He listened to the message. No change with Dillon.

≈

Afternoon found Monty dragging a stack of newspapers through the front door, mentally calculating how many would fit into the trunk of his rental car. All at once, he had a feeling he was being watched.

A man stood on the sidewalk wearing a heavy flannel shirt and dirty work boots. His head was pear-shaped, with large black glasses.

Monty figured it was one of his mother's friends who wanted to offer his condolences. He gave the stranger a sad smile and tried to slide the stack with his feet while holding the screen door open. It'd be a lot easier to throw the papers out, but Maura was a merciless recycler and the habit had worn off on him.

When he looked up again, the man was still standing on the sidewalk, watching.

"Monty Creel?" he said. "Is that you?"

"Hi, hello," Monty said, trying to strike the right balance between familiarity and fuck-off.

"Carl Nelson," the man said. "Roosevelt High. Class of '94."

"Carl Nelson," Monty said, summoning astonishment. They'd probably exchanged all of ten words with each other in high school. Different circles—a Venn diagram with almost no overlap.

"Hey," Carl offered, "you remember that time we ditched Mr. Dolan's P.E. class and went to Tom McKay's house to smoke one of his dad's cigars?"

Monty was certain the memory belonged to someone else, but he smiled and nodded politely. Carl began walking across the lawn, killing any hope Monty had of keeping the encounter brief.

"I was just cleaning up," Monty said.

"I heard." Carl perched a foot on the first porch stair. "Can't tell you how sorry I am." His voice clenched. His eyes were red and rimming. This stranger felt worse about Monty's mother than Monty did.

"Thanks. That means a lot."

"I heard it happened right inside there." Carl stepped up onto the porch and peered in.

"That's what they told me."

"Life, man. So fragile, isn't it?" He bit his lip and lowered his head. He stood there, unmoving.

Monty wasn't sure what to do. "Did you want to come in for a minute?" he offered.

Carl stepped over the threshold and into the living room. He sat down on the couch and propped his work boots on the coffee table. The glass top looked like it might shatter under the weight.

"I've been out of touch for a while, Carl. Did you know my mother?"

Carl looked at the walls on either side of the room. Something about his face had changed in the last few seconds. "Not really," he said. "I do know your brother pretty well, though."

Monty felt a sharp tingle shoot through his fingertips.

"I probably don't have to tell you Simon isn't the most reliable person in the world," Carl said. "He was supposed to leave something for me. There should've been a key."

The two men faced each other across the living room. Neither of them spoke. The moment took on physical properties—density, mass, boundaries. Monty knew there was a simple way to end this standoff: give this guy the Ziploc bag and be done with it. There was no reason it had to go on a minute longer. But an anger had been ignited in him and he wasn't ready to let it go out.

"I know what you're looking for," Monty said. "It's gone. I threw it away this morning, with the first load of garbage I took to the dump."

Carl's nostrils flared. "If you're telling me the truth, that's going to be a problem."

The doorbell rang. Carl's eyes cut to the front of the house.

"Hold on," Monty said.

When he opened the door, he saw a thin woman with gray hair pulled back in an efficient-looking ponytail. "Mr. Creel, I'm Sandy Jenkins. We spoke yesterday about the estate." Her voice struck a note of practiced gravity. "Is now a good time to get started?"

Behind her was a short man with the build of a bear, and a clipboard in one hand. "Um," Monty said, "why not?" He opened the door to let them in. "The place is kind of a mess. I'd hoped to have it in better shape."

The pair looked around, instantly assessing.

When Monty turned back to the living room, Carl was gone. He heard the sound of the back door closing quietly. Monty raced to the kitchen and looked out the window just in time to see Carl slip through the back gate.

"Mr. Creel," Sandy Jenkins called, "are you there? Shall we get started?"

"I'm sorry," he said, returning to the living room. "So how does this work?"

"It's up to you," she said. "We understand there's a lot of emotions at a time like this. Obviously there's things you'll want to keep, for sentimental reasons. You can be involved in this process as much as you'd like."

Monty looked around the house, at the faded prints on the walls, the fake ferns hanging in the window. He could not summon one good memory of this place.

"Sell everything you can," he said. "Throw the rest away."

≈

"Where are you?" he asked.

There was a moaning sound on the other end. "Emergency room," Maura said. "Dillon's fever spiked. Doctor said to bring him in."

Monty's hand clenched the steering wheel. "What are they saying?"

"We've been waiting over an hour and no one's seen him yet."

"What?" He'd been driving around aimlessly since leaving the estate sale people at his mother's house. Now he pulled over to the side of the road.

"This place is a shit-show," Maura said. "A fucking disaster."

Sitting in his rental car alone, Monty felt worse than helpless—he felt responsible.

"Let me talk to someone," he said.

"No, Monty."

"Put me on with someone. Give the phone to whoever's in charge."

He could hear her talking.

Then: "Hello." It was a woman's voice, at once officious and desultory.

"Do you have any idea how long my son has been waiting to see someone?"

"Sir, I'm not—"

"He needs medical attention."

"We have a lot of sick people that need attention, sir."

"I don't care how many people there are. Only one of them is my son."

"If you were here you'd see how busy we are."

Monty's ears began to buzz. "Do you understand what it means to suffer?" he whispered.

"Excuse me?" she said.

"One of these days," he said to the woman, "someone's going to show you what pain really is."

He heard the line click. The buzzing in his ears receded. He waited ten minutes for Maura to call him back. When she didn't, he texted: *Sorry.*

≈

The sign out front said "Shooters Tavern." He'd never been here before, but he knew this area of town. It was an industrial corridor, south of the frontage road.

Monty parked the car on the street and went in. The place was as big and welcoming as a bus terminal, so new it smelled more like a construction site than a club. It wasn't late, but the place was snarled with people, starting at the bar and stretching to the far walls. There was a stage to the rear set up for a band.

Monty took a position against the wall. It was a saggy pants and baseball cap crowd. He was easily the oldest person here.

"What are you drinking?" A cocktail waitress with a trim body balanced a serving tray on one hand.

"Whiskey and soda," Monty said.

She eyeballed him. This was not the kind of place for that drink, but he knew he'd look more foolish if he switched, so he nodded and went back to scanning the room.

Monty knew he'd come here because it was the type of bar Simon might frequent. But he was less certain why he was bothering to look for him at all. Spite? Anger? Probably. Or maybe he was here simply to find out why he still felt the need to see him.

"Four bucks." The waitress was back. How she managed to surf her way through this thicket of people with a tray of drinks was beyond Monty.

He pulled out a ten and gave it to her, nodded to keep the change. He drank until the ice slid against his nose. A trickle of perspiration ran down his spine.

When the band walked on stage, the crowd instinctively moved towards it, iron filings drawn to a magnet. Then he glimpsed a face he recognized. It had been four years, but he still saw something he knew in that face: himself, only thinner, paler, older.

A moment later, the band buzzed to life—whining guitars; mumbled, inaudible lyrics. Simon was watching the band but didn't seem to be enjoying himself, wasn't swaying or patting his chest the way everyone else was.

Monty allowed himself to edge closer until he stood right behind his brother. He leaned over his shoulder and spoke.

"I found the bag you hid in the bedroom." Monty wasn't sure why this was the first thing he said to his brother after so much time, but he knew immediately it was a poor choice.

Simon didn't move for a few seconds. Then he bolted—threading and shoving his way toward an emergency exit. It wasn't until Simon had nearly made it to the door that Monty decided to give chase.

The air was cold outside. He was in some kind of alley, and he just caught sight of his brother as he cut around the edge of the building.

"Simon!" he called out after him.

But Simon was already gone. When Monty reached the front, he saw his brother running down the center of the street. Then, perhaps realizing how exposed he was, Simon veered off the road and threw himself at a chainlink fence.

Monty reached him before he could scramble over. He grabbed his shirt and yanked him down. Simon fell into a heap in the gravel.

"You fucking idiot!" Monty yelled, standing over him.

Simon looked woozy. His head lolled, and his hair hung in a curtain over his eyes.

"Why are you running from me?" Monty asked.

"Isn't it obvious?"

"I wanted to see you."

"Why? So you could feel superior?" Simon's voice was raspy. "I hope you're not disappointed."

"I can't say I'm surprised." A train whistle blew somewhere in the near distance. A shaky roar began to vibrate the ground. "Mom's dead. Did you even know that?"

"I need the key," Simon said. "The one in the bag. You can keep the rest but I need that key."

"Did you hear me? She's dead."

Simon started to pick himself up off the gravel. "I know," he said. "I was there."

"You were?" The train was loud now and still growing.

"Of course I was. I was there when she died and I stayed with her until the paramedics showed up."

"But why—" The train's roar was so ferocious now there was no point talking, and the question—whatever it was—didn't seem worth asking once it had passed.

"I'm not really popular with the local authorities," Simon said. "But you probably could've guessed that."

"What's wrong with you?" Monty asked.

Simon shook his head. "This place, this town. It maims you. It doesn't even have the decency to kill you."

Monty knew this was the best answer his brother could give. "Forget I asked," he said. "All I want is help with Mom. We have responsibilities."

Simon looked at Monty sharply. "That's why you chased me down?"

"Why else would I bother?"

"Good point," Simon said with a sneer. He began to dust himself off. "You know, Mom was sick for a long time. The woman could barely take care of herself by the end."

"No one told me anything," Monty said, his voice falling flat in the back of his throat.

"Would it have mattered?" Simon laughed.

"Don't," Monty said.

"You made a great life for yourself," Simon said. "But you lost the right to come back and pass judgment on the ones who didn't. Go home."

The words stripped something away, some scab Monty hadn't even been aware of. He could see now what a mistake it had been to come. There was nothing left for him here. He reached into his pocket and pulled out the Ziploc bag. He tossed it to Simon, who seized it with both hands and began inspecting the contents. Monty turned and started walking back to where he'd parked.

"Thanks, brother," Simon called out, but the words were barely audible.

Monty was floating on a dark and tenuous orbit. He felt the kind of total isolation that threatens to rob you of your own identity. Yes, he had a wallet with ID and credit cards, even a picture of his kids, but he honestly couldn't say who he was at that moment.

He made it to the car, just managed to unlock it and let himself in. He closed the door. He sat for a moment. He looked at his phone. Four missed calls, all of them from Maura. He hit Send.

After the third ring, he prepared himself for voicemail, but when the line stopped ringing it was her. In one word, *Hello,* he could feel the tiredness in her voice—exhausted from all she'd gone through with the kids, the fever, the emergency room. The sound stung him. He started crying, lightly at first, but it grew until his whole body was shaking.

"What's the matter?" she asked, her voice suddenly alert, tender.

He couldn't answer right away.

"Monty," she said. "What's wrong? Tell me."

He forced himself to catch his breath, to be still. The line was so clear it made the distance between them seem like nothing. He could sense her body heat, her pulse, through the phone.

"I need you," he said. "I need you with me."

She didn't say anything for a few moments. And the silence was so perfect and deep he could almost imagine what her next words would be.

The Physics of Floating

In the days leading up to the final weekend of canoe-building there was some uncertainty over who would go, or whether anyone would go at all. My parents took to having this debate in front of Marty and me. In the past, their fights had happened in the bedroom with the door closed, the muffled sounds of their shouts setting us on edge the way a dropping barometer will make farm animals skittish.

To this day, I'm uncertain if it was a tactical decision to lay their arguments before us. When I was younger, I assumed adults did things on purpose, their actions governed by logic and strategy. I knew a lot less about the world back then.

"We don't have anything else to prove, Michael," my mother said. The four of us were at the dinner table. It was the Wednesday before we were supposed to go back to finish the canoe.

"We have *everything* to prove, Jeannie."

Mashed potatoes and string beans were cooling on our plates. Marty had his eyes closed. He was mouthing something to himself. I knew he was trying to will himself into Human Hologram form—to be there without really being there.

"The canoe is basically done," my mother said. "It was a success. You succeeded in showing the world what a success you are."

"What a success *we* are," my dad corrected her. "But what's the point in building a canoe ninety percent of the way?"

"I'm sorry," my mother said. "Remind me what's the point of building a canoe at all."

My father shook his head and looked at me as if I might be on his side, which I was, but would never say out loud.

"Given everything that's happened," my mother said, "don't you think it's at least a little morbid?"

Dad was still looking at me when she said this, so I saw the color drain from his face.

When he turned back to my mother, he was squeezing the napkin in his lap. "I don't want to live our lives like we're afraid of anything."

"Fear? You think this is about being afraid?" She shook her head. "Sometimes I wonder how you could be so dense."

"Denseness is a choice," my dad said quietly. "Being dense might be the only goddamn way I'm going to survive this."

My father was, in many ways, a petulant child. It was a characteristic that tended to bring out a joylessness in my mother, made her play a role she didn't like. But I could tell she'd understood what he'd said, and maybe appreciated it. Part of her wanted to finish that canoe as well. It was just a part of her that was hidden behind a lot of the other parts.

One week earlier had been the two-year anniversary of my sister's accident. My mother marked the occasion by boxing up the things in Collette's bedroom and dropping them off at Goodwill. She made Marty and I help, and afterwards she gave us each ten dollars.

"Did you want to go anywhere to spend it?" she asked as we pulled out of the Goodwill parking lot.

"Ice cream!" Marty shouted from the backseat.

"Baskin Robbins or Mr. Softee's?"

"Baskin has more flavors," Marty said.

"But Softee's has chocolate dip," I pointed out. "And sprinkles."

"They're pretty far apart," my mother said. "So you'll have to pick one."

We settled on Mr. Softee's. Afterwards we sat on the bench looking out at the parking lot. Cars prowled the lanes, looking for spots. People went into and out of the Safeway next door. Marty got a cookie cone, even though I told him regular cones could hold more ice cream. My mother got a small cup of vanilla and ate with us. We hadn't spent this much time alone with her in months.

"I don't think we should have gotten rid of Collette's things," Marty said.

"It was time," my mother said. She broke off a piece of her Styrofoam cup and put it into her mouth to chew on.

"Time for what?" Marty asked.

"I don't know," she murmured. "It's something people say. I thought I should say it."

Two teenaged boys climbed out of a pickup and walked across the parking lot toward us. They were wearing baseball uniforms. Their cleats made a metallic clinking sound on the asphalt. For some reason, I felt embarrassed to be sitting with my mother and little brother.

"What about you?" my mother asked me.

"About me what?"

"Do you think we should have gotten rid of Collette's things?"

"We didn't get rid of all of it."

"Oh really?"

"I kept her record player. And Marty kept her giraffe brush."

My mother didn't say anything. She spit the chewed-up piece of Styrofoam into her cup.

"We wanted something to remember," Marty said.

"It's no different than you keeping her ashes," I said.

My mother turned to me, a look of betrayal on her face. "You knew?"

My mom had put Collette's ashes in the trunk of her car shortly after we'd gotten them back from the funeral home. They were still in the green cardboard box they came in, nestled between the spare tire and a set of golf clubs that belonged to my father. I didn't think it was a big secret.

The teenaged boys emerged from Mr. Softee's and sat on the curb nearby. They kept looking over at us in a way I didn't like.

"You should have told me," my mother said. I wasn't sure if she was talking about the things of Collette's we'd kept, or the fact that we knew where her ashes were.

"Marty and I aren't ready to move on like you are," I said.

"I've tried everything," she said, a note of pleading in her voice. "You can see that, can't you? I've tried everything."

"There's always something else to try," I said.

My mother sighed and looked out at the parking lot again. Heat waves were beginning to rise from the surface. "Raise crows," she said, "and eventually they'll peck out your eyes."

≈

By the last weekend on the Upper Peninsula there were only two families left, us and the Wetzels. It was strange that we'd spent so much time with them, so many weekends engaged in the singular pursuit of building a canoe, yet we'd hardly spoken to each other.

I knew Mr. Wetzel worked in Chicago and their daughters' names were Kathleen, Roberta and Vera. Roberta was about my age, Kathleen a few years older, and Vera closer to Marty's age.

That first morning we found our canoes upside down on wooden sawhorses. For the first time, we could see all the stitching we'd done, all the patches to the bark. It was a thing held together entirely through tension. Everything pushing against everything equally, a taut balance. We'd bent this wood and shaped this hull. We'd built it with our hands.

"How does it work?" Marty asked as we walked around our canoe.

"What do you mean?" I asked.

"How's it going to hold us? In the water?"

"It's called displacement," my dad said. He was thrilled to see the culmination of our work. "Simple physics. You'll see."

My mother didn't say anything. She just ran her fingers over the jackpine stitching, the way you might examine an old and healing wound.

Big Angus was wearing an olive barn jacket and a heavy flannel shirt. There was a slight chill in the morning air, but it would soon be sweltering beneath the tree canopy.

"Now we come to the end of the journey," he said. "Or as I like to call it, the moment of truth." He looked around at us, expecting a laugh.

"We're gonna need some folks to collect some things today," he continued. "First off is the black spruce pitch. In the olden days, it was the job of the first born to go looking for it."

Big Angus pointed at Kathleen and me. "I'll show you where to find it."

It felt odd to be singled out. I half-expected my parents to intervene, but they stepped aside. Hesitantly, Kathleen and I followed Big Angus as he made his way deeper into the forest. The ground got wetter, the air swampier.

"What you're looking for is something like this." He pointed at a black blob growing from a knot on the side of a pine tree. The blob was hard and crusted. "Take a stick and knock it off, like so. And collect them in this here sack."

He held out a worn burlap sack. When Kathleen didn't make a move for it, I took it.

"They grow best toward the bottom of the trunk."

"What's everyone else doing while we're stuck doing this?" Kathleen asked.

Big Angus smiled. "Eugene's putting them to good work."

"How much of this stuff do we have to get?"

Big Angus made a vague gesture and said, "Collect the amount of a pregnant woman's belly." He turned and headed back toward the clearing where the others were. "Better get to work."

When he was gone, I said, "I'm Jack," because I doubted she knew my name.

"So it's you and me, Jack," Kathleen said, and marched off deeper into the woods. I threw the sack over my shoulder and followed her.

Kathleen Wetzel was what most people would call a tomboy. She had short, feathery hair, and well-defined muscles in her arms and legs. She was wearing a Def Leppard t-shirt and cutoff jeans.

"How old are you?" I asked, trying to keep up.

"Old enough to be your sister," she said without looking back. "So don't get any funny ideas."

She knelt down near the base of a tree. "Here's one." She knocked the black blob off and picked it up to inspect it. "Incoming," she said, tossing it my way.

I wasn't expecting the throw, and missed it, badly.

"Do you believe in the universe, Jack?" When she looked at me, her eyes were gray and unreadable.

"As a place?"

"Like connections and intersections. Like there's a plan and a reason for things."

"I never thought about it like that," I said.

"Or do you think stuff just happens independent of each other?"

"Isn't that how things work? In real life?"

"I was reading a study that said people who believe in a higher power live, like, twenty years longer than people who don't. I read a lot of studies," she said. "It's kind of my thing." She knocked off another piece of pitch and handed it to me. "I hope there's a meaning to the universe. Like you and me getting stuck with this stupid job. What if something is supposed to happen? Then blah, blah, blah, twenty years from now we'll still remember what happened in the woods that day we got sent out to collect tree poop for our stupid family canoes."

She knelt near another tree and pried off a big piece of pitch.

"That would be something," I said.

"I'm fifteen," she said. "I'm going to be a sophomore."

I had turned twelve the month before, but it seemed important that I not tell her my age.

We worked in silence for a while—Kathleen knocking the pitch off the trees and me carrying the bag. When it grew heavy on my shoulder, I bunched up all the pitch, but we only had about half of what we'd need.

"Hey," Kathleen said, "I gotta take a leak. Turn around."

I did as she asked.

"No peeking," she said. "Don't be a perv."

I heard her work the zipper on her cutoffs. A moment later, I heard a stream splashing against the forest floor. A slight breeze kicked up, making the hairs on my forearms stand on end.

"All done," she said. "Thanks for being a gentleman."

"Why did your family decide to build a canoe?" I asked.

"I'm not sure why anyone does anything."

"Mine did it because my sister died. At least that's what I think."

"I could tell something was wrong with your family." She handed me another piece of pitch. "Are your parents going to get divorced?"

As bad as things had been since Collette's death, I'd never considered this possibility before. But now that she'd mentioned it, it seemed like the only realistic outcome.

"I hope I didn't bust your bubble," she said. "You look like I might've bust your bubble."

"I've got something in my eye," I said. "That's all."

"I read a study somewhere that said, like, ninety percent of parents who lose a child end up getting divorced."

I didn't say anything.

"Don't worry. My parents got divorced too. That's my stepmom. And my sisters are stepsisters. Families are fucked up these days. They're like dandelions after they turn white. A little puff of wind comes up and everyone scatters. Just floating along on their own breeze. That's the way of the world. Nothing you can do about it."

I said, "Thanks, that makes me feel better," even though it didn't.

I desperately wanted to be done with this job. I wanted to be back with my family, while it was still intact.

We kept collecting pitch. The burlap made my skin itch.

"How much do we have," Kathleen asked.

She snatched the bag from me and slid it under her t-shirt.

"Oh my God," she said, cradling it in both hands. "I'm pregnant. I told you to use protection. Now we have to tell my parents. I want to keep it."

"Shut up," I said.

"Are you going to live up to your responsibilities, Jack? You know, this means we'll have to get married."

"Give me the bag back."

She slid the bag out from underneath her shirt and tossed it back to me. "God, you're no fun, Jack. NFJ—that's what you are. I got stuck out here with a real NFJ."

"I didn't like the joke," I said.

"You need to lighten up, NFJ. Try greeting the world with a smile. It might improve your outlook."

We both looked around at where we were.

"That's enough tree poop," she said. "If Angus thinks we need more, he can haul his own ass out here and get it."

≈

By the time we got back to the clearing, Big Angus had started a fire with a large steaming pot suspended over it, like a witch's cauldron.

"The eldest have returned," Big Angus said. "We've been expecting you."

Both families were sitting on log benches around the fire. Their hands were black and their faces were smudged with soot. Whatever tasks they'd done, it didn't look like they'd been working as hard as we had.

I gave the sack of pitch to Big Angus, and he dropped it into the boiling pot. The burlap slowly soaked and sank to the bottom where we couldn't see it anymore.

"Now what?" my dad asked.

Big Angus didn't say anything, just stood over the kettle.

"What was that girl like?" Marty asked when I sat next to him.

"Mostly annoying," I said.

"Whoa!" It was Mr. Wetzel who said it, and everyone looked back at the pot.

The pitch had turned into liquid and was seeping through the fibers of the burlap sack. Brown globs of pitch floated to the surface. Big Angus began scooping it out and dropping it into a plastic bucket. At the same time, Eugene started sifting what looked like ground-up charcoal into the bucket and stirring it all together.

"This here is your sealant," Big Angus said. "This'll make sure no water can get in through those seams in your canoe. But you gotta be quick because once this stuff dries, it's forever."

We followed Eugene over to the canoes where he showed us how to apply it with a flat stick.

It got really quiet as we all set about the task. I think because we'd had to do so many difficult things over the course of the summer, we were thrilled at the prospect of throwing ourselves into this. Big Angus and Eugene stood back and watched.

≈

The next morning I woke up to find Marty staring at me over the lip of his sleeping bag.

"What's displacement?" he asked. I could tell he'd been biting at his lips.

"What are you talking about?" I asked.

"Dad said that's what'll make us float. The canoe with all of us on it."

"I'm not sure what displacement is. But I've seen canoes float before."

"What if ours won't?"

"I guess we have to trust Big Angus. And maybe Mom and Dad too."

I was expecting Marty to mention Collette, but he didn't. Which I think showed progress, so I said, "We have to trust people as long as we can trust them."

When we climbed out of the tent, our parents were sitting around the camp stove. They looked up at us and stopped talking, as if we'd caught them saying something they shouldn't have.

"Breakfast is ready," my mom said, standing quickly and heading for the tent to change.

"Better hurry," my dad said. "Big Angus wants us down at the canoes in ten minutes."

Breakfast was instant oatmeal, which neither of us liked, but we were hungry.

"Displacement is when you push against something, like water for instance, and by doing that, it pushes you back, holds you up."

We both looked up at my father.

"I should have explained it earlier," he said.

≈

Big Angus instructed the four of us to each grab a gunwale and lift in unison. I was on Mom's side. Marty was on Dad's. Lifting it off the sawhorses, we felt the full weight of the canoe. It was heavier than I expected. It shifted in our hands, and the momentum almost sent the nose into the ground, but we were able to stabilize it.

"Okay now," Big Angus said. "Start walking toward the shore."

All four of us began to take heel-toe steps. When we emerged from the trees, a gust of wind hit the side of the canoe and sent us scrambling. I felt my shoes sink into the soft sand of the shore, and a moment later I was standing in ankle-deep water.

"Good, set it down there," Angus said.

The hull let out a slap as it hit the water. Then it rested on the surface. I could feel the icy waves biting at my ankles. Big Angus handed us each a wooden paddle. None of us were certain of what would happen next.

"How do we do this, Big Angus?" my dad asked.

"This is the easiest part of all," he said.

"What if it tips over?" Marty asked.

No one responded.

Big Angus waded out into the water to stand with us, but he didn't touch our canoe. "Mom and Dad, you keep it steady for the boys while they climb in. There. That's good."

Sitting in the canoe, I could feel it bounce on the choppy water. My hands grew slick with sweat. I wanted to jump out.

"Now, Mom, you go. Swing your leg over the edge, then slide your weight over. Yeah. Like that."

The only thing holding us steady was my dad. The breeze felt more forceful. The canoe kept bucking sideways.

"All right, Dad. Now it's your turn."

"The wind's too strong," my dad said. "And the current's all wrong."

Marty braced his hands against the sides of the boat.

"Take two steps, and climb in. No hesitation. Let the vessel do the work," Big Angus said. "There's a trick to it, but the trick is to just do it."

"Oh God," my mother whispered. She was gripping her paddle so hard her knuckles were white.

My dad took three deep breaths. The canoe surged forward. When he started to climb in, it listed toward the starboard side. The lip of the canoe neared the waterline. But then he was in and the canoe righted itself and we were gliding over the surface of the water.

"That's it?" my mom asked. "You're in, Michael? You're with us?"

"I'm in," my dad said. "We're all in."

"Now paddle on opposite sides," Big Angus called from the shore.

We dipped our paddles into the water and rowed, and the bow split the water and we left a wake behind us. We were loose, untethered. The buoyancy of the canoe on the water was the closest I'd ever felt to flying. All four of us rowed for a few minutes without talking.

The mosquitos still buzzed. Birds cawed and dove. Water lapped at the hull. Overhead a plane streaked across the sky with a hundred people going somewhere important. But in that moment, we were locked in, and nothing else mattered.

Then I looked up and saw that we were far out from the shore. Big Angus and Eugene and the Wetzels seemed tiny, like a memory that's barely even a memory anymore.

"We might not want to go too far," my mother said. Her voice sounded distant and dreamy.

"You're right," my dad said. "Not today, at least."

Publication History

Versions of some of these stories have appeared in the following publications:

"What We Build Upon the Ruins" – *Identity Theory*

"Boy in the Bubble" – *Literal Latte*

"Coyote in the City" – *Underground Voices*

"Eureka, California" – *Swill Magazine*

"3 Out of 5 Stars" – *Adirondack Review*

"Those Who Trespass" – *Word Riot*

"Ling" – *Zouch Magazine*

"Homefront" – *The Pleasure You Suffer: A Saudade Anthology*

Acknowledgments

Countless people have played a part in shaping these stories over the years. I will try to credit a few of them here.

First off, a big thanks to the helpful people at the Museum of Ojibwa Culture in St. Ignace, Michigan, where I first learned about the construction of birchbark canoes.

I'd also like to thank the teachers who have looked at these works and provided insight, even when there wasn't much hope they'd ever grow up to be real stories: Ernest Hebert, Richard Peabody, Kevin Canty, Deirdre McNamer, and Debra Magpie Earling. I've also benefitted from having some incredible readers over the years: Alex Shapiro, Dave Cohen, Penelope Whitney, and Joe Campana.

There's another group of people deserving gratitude who fall into a category I might comfortably label Guru: Adam Skilken, Tony Lipp, Ben Tanzer, Joe Peterson, and Stephen Kahn.

The members of the band Even Less Dignity deserve special recognition for the sheer amount of ass they routinely kick: Zak Andersen, Pat Bousliman, Jeff Forbes, Jim Messina, and Scott Olsen.

My family, always, for saying yes. Brent Sr, Dorothea, Brent Jr, Taya, Millie, and Reed.

The fact that you are holding this book in your hands is due in large part to the wisdom and faith of Jerry Brennan, the best editor I've ever worked with, and one of Chicago's finest writers to boot.

Lastly, of course, immeasurable thanks go to my wife Natalie, who emotionally subsidizes my writing, and without whom I don't think I could have done this, nor wanted to.

About the Author

Giano Cromley is the author of the novel *The Last Good Halloween*, which was a finalist for the High Plains Book Award. He is the chair of the Communications Department at Kennedy-King College, and he lives on the South Side of Chicago with his wife and two dogs.

About Tortoise Books

Slow and steady wins in the end, even in publishing. Tortoise Books is dedicated to finding and promoting quality authors who haven't yet found a niche in the marketplace—writers producing memorable and engaging works that will stand the test of time.

Learn more at www.tortoisebooks.com.

CPSIA information can be obtained
at www.ICGtesting.com
Printed in the USA
BVOW03s2108061117
499691BV00001B/38/P